Southern Fried
LIES

SUSAN SNOWDEN

Archer Hill

Archer Hill Publishing
Columbia, South Carolina

Copyright © 2012 by Susan Cozart Snowden

Excerpts from this novel first appeared in slightly different form in the following publications: *moonShine review* (as "Reunion"), Anne Hicks, ed.; and *Christmas Presence*, an anthology (as "A Hair-Raising Holiday"), Celia Miles and Nancy Dillingham, eds.

Cover art: *Lamia* 2008 © Randy Siegel. Acrylic on wooden panel (www.RandySiegelArt.com)

Cover and text design by Tomas Grignon

Archer Hill Publishing
P.O. Box 23341
Columbia, SC 29224-3341
www.archerhillpublishing.com

Printed in the United States of America

ISBN 978-0-9853301-0-1
Library of Congress Control Number: 2012908846

For my parents, in memoriam

Southern Fried
LIES

The snaky blue lines on my legs are no reason to cut school. The running sores have sealed up, and just because the new skin over them is shiny is not a good excuse to miss more time. Yesterday my mother informed me I had to go back, but this morning I know I'm still not ready. I've convinced Mother, the warden, that I'm dizzy and she's granted me a stay of execution.

"Can we at least crack these blinds, Sarah? It's like a tomb in here. There, now. Would you like a little Coke on crushed ice? Do you feel upsy?"

"No, I'm not *upsy*." Why is she talking baby-talk?

"A little bouillon might—"

"Mother, please."

I'm flat on my back, blanket up to my nose. Because I'd planned to drag myself out to the horrible Howell School, I rolled my hair last night. One Minute Maid orange juice can on the top, one on each side, and one at the nape of my neck. The two metal clippies anchoring the can on the back apparently failed in the night; that can—the most tortuous to sleep on—had come undone. My wrist *thunks* against it as I reach up to cover my eyes.

For some reason Mother doesn't comment on my smart-aleck tone, but I feel her hovering over me and brace myself. A rustle beside my pillow, then a click. She has scooped up the loose can and set it on the bedside table.

"You're not the least bit feverish."

Her palm on my forehead is cool, caring. Nurse Clara Barton, tending the sick.

When she leaves to "run errands" I roam the house. Etha Mae, our maid, has already cleaned my parents' room, so I tiptoe to Mother's closet along the vacuum tracks. It would be like her to measure a footprint to determine who has trespassed. I open the door and stare at the disaster. No one in Atlanta who knows Catherine Claiborne would believe it: stylish Bleyle knits, gowns for gala balls, cashmere sweaters in sherbet colors crammed alongside ragged pedal pushers and stained, faded camp shirts. Shoes slung in on the floor, summer spectators mixed up with suede pumps, a jumble of heels and toes.

Anyone acquainted with Mother—especially members of the Dogwood Garden Club and the Rabun Gap Guild—would be shocked to see this. They would imagine neat rows of pumps lined up according to color. Garments draped on cushiony, satin-covered hangers, evenly spaced to avoid wrinkling.

I'm not sure what I'm looking for, but I'm compelled to go through her things, rifle through her drawers. I'm like Sergeant Friday; he's always looking for a clue, but he doesn't know what it is till he finds it.

My eyes sting, probably from the stale Chanel No. 5 puffing out at me from the packed outfits. I close the door, gently, hoping a precarious hat box won't crash down. This closet is a balancing act. Do not disturb.

The house is graveyard quiet except for Etha Mae's humming in the kitchen. I wander to the living room, sit down at Mother's Queen Anne secretary, and ease out the big middle drawer where she's stuck months of Sav-a-Stamp booklets on top of family photographs. I sift through snapshots and stop on an oversize picture. We are all there, posed, all six of us: Daddy, Ben, Annie and me, Mother holding Chris. We're dressed up, gathered in the garden, Mother's proud Paul's Scarlet roses in the background. We look soft in sepia tones. Serene. This is just the way a "nice" Atlanta family should look. Maybe it's Easter Sunday and they're going to church, you might think. Lovely. But if you looked hard, if you were a curious person, you would wonder why everyone isn't looking at the camera. You'd think, hmm, they're smiling their say-cheese smiles, but for some reason the mother is cutting her eyes at the oldest boy. Has he said something she doesn't like? Her mouth *is* turned up at the corners, but . . . is that a smirk?

I know the answer, but this is still the best picture I can find of my family, and it's the one I'll take with me if I decide to leave. Because this time it will be far away, for good.

Now I really am dizzy, so I'm going back to bed. I have to act sick for Mother anyway, and she'll be roaring up the driveway any minute in her new Buick. The car actually drives her; it's too powerful, but Daddy bought it for her—"to perk her up," he said—after the Thanksgiving disaster.

I stop at Chris's room on the way back to mine and sit on the floor by his toy chest, doodling on the Majik Easel, his favorite thing right now. By next week it'll be different. It'll be a box turtle or a hand puppet. I print "Sarah Claiborne" neatly on the plastic page, then lift it slowly and watch the letters disintegrate.

"Don't you want some lunch, Miss Sarah?"

"No thanks, Mae. I'm not hungry."

"Lawd have mercy, Miss Sarah, you gon' get weak."

"OK, I'm coming."

Poor Etha Mae. She always senses when something is going on in our house, but she never gets details. I don't give them to her because I can't stand to see her face all worried. What could she do anyway? She's already got us on three prayer chains at Ebenezer Baptist.

I put the easel back on Chris's shelf. If I could write down the last few years on it, I would. I'd squeeze the whole story on it, in microscopic writing like in those matchbox-size Bibles. Then I could yank up that plastic page and, bingo, a clean slate. I would go back to when I climbed chinaberry trees and mimosas and played kick ball with the neighborhood kids. But if I couldn't fit all that on, I'd at least go back to before my brother Ben left, say 1958, and I'd write a different story.

Part One

Set thine house in order.

The King James Bible, 2 Kings, XX, 1

My best friend, Wendy, referred to our house on Valley View Road as the Atlanta Museum. It was picture-perfect. Every piece of furniture in place, candy dishes filled, fresh flowers arranged just so. A hint of lemon in the air. Odd, some would say, for a house where four kids lived. Not really. We were well-mannered Southern children, Catherine and Edward Claiborne's children. We knew not to prop our dirty feet on the mahogany coffee table, to always plump up the needlepoint pillows when we arose from the Chippendale sofa. And on the occasions when Mother closed a door hard, which she did often, and the Audubon bird paintings shifted out of position, it was second nature for one of us to straighten them.

Annie, my little sister, had no trouble whatsoever with our museum life. She could sit on her bed reading, get up, and with one quick swoop smooth out the dent in the spread; you'd never know she'd been there. She didn't even leave footprints on her pink throw rugs. I, on the other hand, could pass through my room and send movie magazines fluttering, stacks of records toppling. So instead of listening to Mother rant about what a slob I was, I stayed outside as much as possible. Up in a giant chinaberry tree, actually, until I sprouted breasts.

"Sarah Claiborne, this feral behavior must stop," Mother would say. "You're a young lady now."

"What's 'feral'?" I asked, knowing her answer.

"Look it up."

After that I started slipping upstairs to the attic to draw or read or just daydream. It was comfortable up there, although I had to lie on an army cot with a musty mattress. But it was nothing like a museum. I hid my copy of *Peyton Place* in the cedar closet and could pull it out any time to read the best parts.

Clunky Chris, the baby of our family, survived by tinkering with his toy trains in the cellar, or hanging around in the garage doing who-knows-what. It was my older brother, Ben, who had it pretty easy. He stood up to Mother one day, told her he didn't want anyone in his room—not even to clean. It was out and out war for a while, but he finally won; I don't know how. Anyway, he stayed holed up in there after school listening to Broadway show music and reading books on UFOs. I was the only one who knew what went on there, in what Mother called the "inner sanctum," because every night he let me come in for a while.

We'd head back to his room after dinner to talk about Mother, what she'd said, how she'd acted. Dinner was her time to capture us for a half hour and grill us.

"Do you plan to practice tonight, Sarah?" (Meaning practice the piano for my lesson the next day.)

"Annie, what did they serve in the cafeteria today?" (Meaning, did you cheat on your diet, Miss Chubby Cheeks?)

Daddy and Chris didn't get questioned. Oh, Chris got corrected on his table manners, and Daddy got assigned after-dinner chores. But it was Ben she fired most of her questions at—and complaints. It seemed like dinner hour at the Claibornes' had two main characters: Mother and Ben. The rest of us were there just to watch the play.

Mother didn't like the way Ben played his role. She'd ask him something and he'd fiddle around with his food and go "un-huh" and "umm" and "nope."

"What? I can't hear you, Ben. Don't mumble. Do you need the car Friday? Have you got a date with Connie? Is there a dance? You didn't bring *The Spokesman* home this week. Have you written another communist essay you don't want us to see?"

When she wasn't gathering information like Lois Lane, she was lecturing him on what he should and shouldn't be doing. She said writing for the school newspaper was wasting his "gift." He should sign up for the literary magazine. In fact, he should be editor.

Ben was so funny. His eyes would get glassy. "I look at her face but I unfocus," he told me. "All I see is a blur."

He could handle her, I guess, because he knew how to give a tiny bit of information during the question-answer part of the play, just enough to shut her up. But then she started going through his stuff, looking through his drawers. He never actually caught her, but he knew what she was doing; he'd found things out of place. That's when he bought the lock for his door.

My father's part in the dinner theater was to hang his head. He'd been at the office all day making money to pay for Mother's orders of special things, like French wallpaper with birds and flowers, and I guess he was too tired to do much but feed himself and do the urgent repair work Mother wanted done—put the kitchen drawer back on the track, unstick the window in the study, whatever. After that he'd nod off in the big wing chair; he could sleep sitting straight up.

After dinner, Mother would crash pans around in the kitchen, then disappear into their bedroom. I can't tell you what she did back there because we weren't allowed to "disturb" her.

Thankfully, my parents went out most Saturday nights, and we could have fun: slop up the kitchen making Chef Boyardee pizza from a box, bring bed pillows in and watch TV on the floor. Ben was like a camp counselor; he could organize Chris and Annie in a snap, get them in the basement making hand puppets out of Annie's old dolls' heads and flannel from outgrown pajamas, or direct them in productions of Flash Gordon. Annie played the evil Ming, marching around in a long, black cape. She would tie Chris in a lawn chair with clothesline and hold him hostage for hours, although she would leave one of his hands free to fan her with a mimosa frond.

While they were engaged in their theatrics, Ben and I escaped to the living room and created zany musical soap operas. My job was to write down the story line—mostly Ben's ideas—and he improvised background music on the piano.

"OK, Sarah, how 'bout this: Edwin, a Fuller Brush salesman, falls in love with Lorna. She hates his brushes, so he buys her perfume."

"Yeah . . . okay."

"It's called Everything."

"Huh?"

"The perfume. Listen: Women who have Everything are happee, contented. (Treble trill on the piano.) She will love me . . . when she smells this . . . oh I know it."

Then I came in. "Oh, Mr. Brush Man, your brushes hurt me. They are so STIFF." I wailed this out, swooning against the piano.

"My dear Miss Lorna, please don't be downcast. I've brought you per-fume . . . that you'll adore!"

"Oh, oh," I squeaked. "Let me smell it!" I mimed opening a bottle, sniffed loudly, nostrils flared.

Ben pounded out major chords with each word: "How . . . do . . . you . . . like . . . it?"

I, Lorna, gagged, then collapsed to the floor.

Annie and Chris didn't understand our shows. One night they came galumphing in from the garage, Chris in his slave garb—underpants and an Indian headband—and Annie in her Ming cape and eyebrow pencil mustache. They wanted us to come watch *their* performance, but we were busy with a tragedy about a librarian who couldn't whisper. We howled and clapped, but they pouted on the sofa.

Timing was important on those nights because we had to wrestle the kids into bed and scramble to get everything shipshape before my parents got home. If my mother came in and discovered her museum in a shambles . . . we didn't want to imagine what would happen.

Uncle Draper and Aunt Alice, who live near Chicago, suddenly appeared one Saturday afternoon. I'd been riding my bicycle up and down our street, bored. Not one of my neighborhood friends was home. I was pedaling past our house for the hundredth time when I spotted their Cadillac, a butterscotch-colored battleship, turning into our driveway. I pulled up next to the car as the power window came down. Cold air blasted out at me; then Uncle Draper's big round face appeared.

"Hey-low, little Sal, how's my girl?" he boomed. He still called me Sally, although no one else had since I was five or six.

I moved out of the way and Uncle Draper unfolded his tall self and got out. He leaned down and gave me a gorilla hug.

"What are y'all doing here?" I asked into his shoulder.

"Headed for Savannah, hon, to see your grandma. Your Uncle Bob and Aunt Bet too."

"But they're in Baltimore."

"Well, sugar, they're driving down for the week; Mama got us a house at the beach. Over at Tybee."

I asked why Jamie, my cousin, wasn't with them.

"He'll come next time, sugar. Mom and Dad home?"

"Sir?"

"Are Catherine and Eddie here?"

"Oh, Mother's here. Daddy's at the office though."

"On Saturday?"

"Just for a little while, I think. Come on in."

Aunt Alice finally got out of the Cadillac, which was almost as wide as our driveway. Uncle Draper went around to help her. She's prissy and she had on high-heel spectator shoes.

"Hello, Sarah, how are you?" No hug, just a pat on my cheek—quick, like I had leprosy.

"I'm fine, thanks."

I led them into the house, through the living room and dining room and into the kitchen. Something had clattered in there so I figured that's where Mother was. I didn't expect to find her on the floor, but there she was on her hands and knees, swabbing up some bubbly brown liquid. Coke, I guess.

"Oh, my god!" she said and jumped up, patting at her hair, which maybe wasn't such a good idea with sticky, wet hands. "What in the—?"

"Hey, sugar!"

My uncle did his King Kong clamp on her while Aunt Alice hung back in the dining room. I was blocking her, so I backed out of the kitchen and zipped outside. I took off on my bicycle, knowing it was rude not to stay and visit with relatives I hadn't seen in ages. But I also knew I was in trouble. Mother hates people to drop by—"unannounced," she calls it—and catch her in her shorts. She wears shorts on weekends, baggy gray ones today with a giant safety pin where the button had come off. I knew I'd be hearing about letting people "barge" in on her like that. But it was my aunt and uncle, all the way from Illinois. What was I supposed to do, tell them to go back home and call for an appointment?

After a kick ball game at Toby Evans', I pedaled home. Daddy's Oldsmobile was on the street, and the big Caddie was gone. I headed down the driveway to park my bike in the garage, but as I rounded the house I heard Mother screaming and doors slamming. Funny, I was on the exact spot where I always stopped after school to listen before going inside. If Mother was in one of her "moods," I wanted to be ready before I walked in—or put off going in as long as I could.

She must be yelling because of me, I thought. She's furious with me for running out on my aunt and uncle.

Huddled against the house, I listened, and whenever I heard a thud or a bump—and once, a shattering noise—I tried to figure out what she'd knocked over or broken. I hoped the TV screen was OK.

"I'm sick of all this, Edward," she shrieked. "Sick, sick, sick. Sick of pretending everything's just fine . . . when it's falling apart (*thump*) like a house of cards."

Daddy said something but I couldn't make out the words.

"I can't take it. Annie's eating herself to death! What am I supposed to do? Put handcuffs on her? (*slam*) Chris won't bathe . . . never sleeps . . . Sarah's out there hanging in trees like a monkey. (*crash*)

"You know, while you're off on your business trips, I'm here trying to deal with your children."

More mumbling from Daddy, maybe his speech about being sorry he had to travel but he was just trying to earn a living.

"Ben's locked away in his room morning and night. There's something seriously wrong with him . . . he has NO friends! (*thump*)

"You have no idea what goes on here, Edward. I can't take it. I won't. I'll end up in Milledgeville!" (*big slam, then quiet*)

I climbed onto my bicycle seat, my heart thumping, and peered in the small, high window at the end of our living room. Chairs were out of their usual spots and the coffee table was on its side. Mother's favorite egg-shaped candy dish—her grandmother's—was shattered. Our rose-beige carpet was littered with sharp porcelain slivers, which Daddy was crawling around picking up. I knew he was thinking about gluing them back together.

When I tiptoed in, he was stacking shards of the dish in a cardboard box.

"Did she have a fight with Aunt Alice?" I asked.

"No, honey."

"Why is she so mad?"

"Darlin', I don't know. She said she was embarrassed for them to see her a mess and our house a mess."

"But it wasn't, Daddy. Chris and his friends left some games out on the front porch, but that was all."

He had his back to me and didn't turn to look at me while he rearranged some books that had flopped over on the shelf.

"Daddy, why did Gram get a beach house and not ask us?"

"Sarah, honey, I need to go back and check on your mother. Why don't you go wash your hands for dinner."

There were no sounds coming from the kitchen.

"What dinner?"

He didn't answer.

My father is an architect and when he can't draw something, sketch it out on paper, he won't discuss it. Now, if our back porch was sagging he would talk about all the possible causes. He would slither under there with a flashlight to pinpoint the trouble. But forget talking to him about something he can't figure out.

I went back to Annie's room, tapped on her door, then poked my head in. She was sitting on the edge of her bed staring at the wall, licking on an Eskimo Pie—real slow. A broken piece of chocolate was falling off the vanilla ice cream part, but her tongue seemed to know on its own to catch it.

"Annie?"

"Mmm."

"Where's Chris?"

"I dunno."

"You okay?"

Nothing.

I closed the door and left her alone. She'd heard the whole thing, I'm sure, including the part about her being fat. Next I went to Ben's door. Just as I started to knock, the door opened. His record player was on, but he had it turned down low.

"Whatcha listenin' to?"

"'Slaughter on Tenth Avenue.' Dinner ready?"

His face told me he knew it wasn't. He turned around and went back to his desk.

"It's *my* fault," I said.

He turned his chair to face me and rolled his eyes.

"Well, I'm the one who invited Uncle Draper and Aunt Alice in, and they caught her in her stupid Lucy Goosies."

"Her what?"

"Those ugly shorts she wears. That's what she calls 'em."

"Sarah, I was here. I saw Uncle Draper and Aunt Alice. I heard the whole fight after they left."

"I let them see her without her fancy clothes. She's mad at me, isn't she?"

"No, she blamed Dad. First she accused him of knowing they were coming and not telling her. She said people don't just 'drop by'

15

Atlanta from Lake Forest, Illinois. Then she started crying. She said Draper makes so much money and they live so much better than we do that Alice looks down on us. She thinks that's why we're never included in their plans."

"What did Daddy say?"

"I couldn't hear."

"We're not poor."

"No, but we don't live like they do."

"They don't care if our house is smaller than theirs. Uncle Draper and Daddy are brothers!"

"Well, something's strange. Mother's right in a way. You know, they never have anything to do with us . . . we haven't seen Uncle Bob and Aunt Bet in three years either."

"Ben, what's Milledgeville?"

"Milledgeville? It's a city. The old capital of Georgia . . . before Atlanta. Why?"

"Mother said she's going to end up there because of us."

"Oh, I get it. The state mental hospital's there. The insane asylum."

"The insane asylum?"

"Forget it, Sarah, she says things like that all the time."

CHAPTER 2

*L*ater that spring Mother announced she was taking Ben on a whirlwind tour of New York City—as an early graduation gift. "You don't seem interested in going to Ft. Lauderdale with your classmates," she pointed out. "So . . . I'm giving you a four-night, five-day trip to the island of Manhattan! I sound like a game show host. Horrors. What do you think, son? The Circle Line boat tour, Broadway shows, the Metropolitan Museum. And of course we'll stay at the Waldorf."

"Mother, Connie wants me to go with her family down to Florida."

"Really, Ben, you can go to a quaint fishing camp in Florida any time. This is an opportunity to expand your mind."

"Can Connie come with us?"

"Ben, I don't feel up to playing chaperone. Here, take these brochures and underline things you're interested in doing—enriching things. Educational. I need to make reservations immediately.

"Why do you have that sullen look on your face? You should be grateful. *I* never had an opportunity like this; you should be ever so grateful you do."

I had figured we'd visit my grandmother in Savannah for spring vacation, especially since she'd gotten a beach house for my aunts and uncles and left us out. Gram's a crotchety old lady and her house is dark and gloomy, but Ben and I never mind visiting her—which we've done every year for as long as I can remember—because it means we can go out to the beach. But this year nobody mentioned Gram or the beach, and not a word was said about me or Annie and Chris going to New York. I wouldn't mind going to the top of the Empire State Building.

I tried to tune out Mother's chatter about the big trip, but I felt sick.

"We're going camping at Red Top Mountain," my friend Wendy said a week before spring break.

"Where's that?"

"North Georgia. It's neat. They've got a lake where you can swim and fish, and there's hiking trails and a pavilion with pinball machines and a jukebox."

"I've never been camping. I mean, not with my family. Isn't it mosquitoey?"

"No! Did you ever swim in a lake in the mountains? It's sooo cold. Ice-cube cold."

"I guess I'll be swimming in Chris's wading pool for my vacation."

Before we left to drive Mother and Ben to Union Station to catch the train, Ben called me into his room and handed me a book. "Don't tell Mother."

"*The Bad Seed*. What's it about?"

"You'll find out. It's strange. You'll like it. We'll talk about it when I get back."

The whole book thing in my family was weird. Mother gave Ben books she said he needed to read. He'd read just enough to get her off his back, then go buy something he wanted. Then he'd give it to me; I'd read it to please him. I hid books Wendy loaned me because I was scared he might tease me about them.

Mother gave Ben a hard time about reading what she called "trash." Once she saw him with a paperback on UFOs and went nuts. "That's fiction, presented as fact, Ben; that's dangerous."

"It's research about UFOs," Ben said, scowling.

Daddy stayed out of book discussions. He read magazines about buildings and the architects who designed them. Now and then he read a book about someone's true-life outdoor adventure, but I never saw him read a novel. Mother told him she gave Ben books so he could discuss them with her. "I need to share my love of reading with *someone*," she said.

My poor father, reminded daily what a disappointment he was. He never said anything back to her.

Mother didn't try to control anybody else's reading habits though; just Ben's. Oh, she took me and Chris and Annie to the library, encouraged us to check out books, but she bought me only two that I can remember. When I was eleven she presented me with Amy Vanderbilt's book on etiquette, and one called *Growing Up*; it had drawings of eyeless babies curled up in little peanut-shaped capsules. When I had questions about the growing up one, she told me to ask Ben. Which I did, but he didn't explain any better than the book.

We never turned on our television the whole time Mother and Ben were in New York. We were all outside a lot. Daddy decided to stay home from the office. "I have a lot of work to do in the yard," he announced that first morning.

I took to the chinaberry tree, knowing Mother would be furious. But she wasn't there to rant, so I hauled *Green Mansions* up to my favorite spot to sit. From up there—high as a two-story house—I could see our whole backyard. At first I watched Daddy raking, and spied on Chris and Annie running around, but then I got absorbed in *Green Mansions*. I figured it would be good to be Rima, the wild "bird girl" in the book. She lived in a shimmery green world where you didn't have to go to school or worry about spring vacations. Then I wondered what Ben was doing that very minute in New York. Maybe he was in one of the points on the Statue of Liberty's crown, looking out over the world, high up like I was.

When I didn't feel like reading, I sunbathed with Annie in Mother's garden. If I couldn't go back to school talking about a trip to New York, I could at least have a mysterious tan.

"Annie, slick some of this on my back."

"What is it?"

"Baby oil with iodine. It'll dye me golden brown."

"Can I use some?"

"I guess . . . but just a little."

I also squeezed some fresh lemon juice on my hair because I have light brown hair that gets streaky blond highlights in the sun—almost white-blond if I use lemon juice. Annie tries to bleach hers too, but it's no use. She's got dark brown hair like my grandmother—Mother's mother. She died when my mother was in high school, but I've seen pictures.

I did get a nice tan and actually stopped hating being at home. Not one door slammed for five days. Chris and Annie never fought. We did what we wanted to do. While we were outside, Etha Mae was inside singing spirituals, not the low-down sad ones, but the hallelu-jah-praise-the-lord ones. She was happy to have us all out of the house so she could strip the old wax off the kitchen floor and polish the brass andirons in the fireplace. She had a long list.

Chris charged in and out of the yard to the woods where he and his buddies were building a fort. Daddy kept a watchful eye on him and burned piles and piles of brush he'd cleared. He fertilized the lawn, separated clumps of liriope between Mother's rose garden and the kids' part of the yard, weeded the flower beds. He loved doing outdoor work.

"It relaxes me, helps me think," he told Mother once when she asked why he didn't hire someone else to do the work. "Clears the cobwebs out of my brain."

We ate anything we wanted to eat. Daddy cooked us a thick steak one night on the grill. Another night we went to my favorite restaurant, Mammy's Shanty, downtown. My father had some papers to pick up at his office, and we stopped there after we stuffed ourselves with fried chicken and the best pecan pie you ever put in your mouth. Mammy's pecan pie is a foot high and most of it is pecans.

On the last night before Mother and Ben came home, Daddy drove us down to the train tracks near Lenox Road. Chris had pestered him to go all week. Chris liked to go around sunset when the Nancy Hanks or the Peach Queen went by. If he was up on Daddy's shoulders, the engineer could spot him, and sometimes he would toot the train whistle.

It was too soon to pick blackberries by the tracks, so Annie and I waited in the car, just sat there enjoying the cool breeze, watching the light around Chris and Daddy turn from gold to blue-gray. It was very still there next to the woods. Cars hardly ever came down that road at night. There was no sound but crickets. Hundreds of them, maybe thousands. Other than that, it was quiet . . . until the train started coming. As it got closer, it seemed to build up speed, and it got louder and louder.

Chris tugged and tugged his make-believe chain in the air, trying to get the engineer to blow the whistle. At first, the man didn't notice, but at the last minute he glanced over, saw Chris, and pulled the whistle—one short blast and one very long one. Chris whooped, shot off Daddy's shoulders, and pitched backwards into the bushes. But he came up grinning.

After Mother and Ben got home, I flipped through the pack of pictures they'd taken—in front of the Waldorf, in Chinatown and Central Park. Funny, Ben looked serious or irritated in the snapshots of him, but Mother looked happy—and pretty. Her hair's thick, sort of a chestnut brown, shoulder length, and in one it's blowing in the wind, and she seems to be laughing. She doesn't look like that at home, I thought. And there was something else odd; she looked young, much younger than my father. He's had silver-gray hair for as long as I can remember. And his wire-rimmed glasses make him look even older.

I was jealous looking at the pictures, but I got over it soon. School let out for summer, the best time of year in my opinion. Seven boys close to my age lived in my neighborhood, explaining why I was a tomboy, I guess, until Mother banned me from backyard sports. In past years we had stayed outside all day playing touch football, baseball, kick ball, and when we got bored with games or constructing forts in the woods, we had pine cone battles. We loaded our bike baskets with pine cones and used garbage can lids as shields. Half of us started at one end of the road, with the others at the opposite end. Somebody would yell "charge" and we'd head for the center, pelting as many of the enemy as possible while warding off blows with our shields. We knew which side had won by tallying wounds.

But two weeks into this summer vacation I was miserable. Wendy was off camping with her family again, and the boys weren't dropping by. I wondered if Mother had sent them an engraved notice saying "Sarah is now participating only in activities for young ladies." Whatever those might be. The boys weren't even around; our street was like one of those cowboy movie scenes where everybody in town cleared out because the bad guys are coming.

"Can I have a friend over?"

"I don't know. *Can* you?" Mother said.

"*May* I?"

"Sarah, we aren't going to make a major production of entertaining you this summer. We have to focus on getting your brother ready for college."

Suddenly I felt nauseous; it hadn't sunk in till that minute that Ben was actually leaving. I remembered a sand castle I'd built at the beach one time. I drizzled water on it and the drops vanished, but when I doused a whole pail on it, it cracked open—like a star burst. That's how my brain felt now. Little mentions of "college" all year must have drip-dropped over my head. But now the big bucket full had come—Ben was leaving!

What would it be like in our house? Who would get grilled at dinnertime? If it was me, who would I talk to afterward? Right now, it seemed as though Ben was already gone. He was always working at Daddy's office, or going off with Connie.

I felt too sick to battle with Mother; I slunk off and stretched out on the glider on our front porch. I lay there staring at the ceiling. I didn't feel like reading, and I wasn't going to ask Annie to play cards.

My favorite game was Canasta, but Annie couldn't hold that many cards.

Suddenly, Rick Stiles was right next to me, his face pressed against the screen. "Whatcha doin'?" he said. "Can you come up to Alder Drive? We need some help."

"Who's 'we'?"

"Me and Tony and Vance."

"What are y'all doing?"

"*Sarah*, can you come?"

"Oh, okay."

Mother had left to go shopping, so why not.

The guys were moving a junked car that old Mrs. Hooper suddenly wanted out of her carport. They wanted to get it down to Rick's parents' garage so they could convert it into a hotrod. They had rolled the thing out into the middle of Alder Drive and were towing it with ropes tied to the front axle. But they'd come to a rise in the road and it wouldn't budge.

"Can you steer while we all pull?" Vance asked. I frowned. "Come on, Sarah. It's gonna take all three of us to get this thing goin'."

There was no front seat, but they'd rigged up an old swing seat so you could sit at the wheel. It's just that there was no top on the car, so I'd be riding in the open air. "Oh, all right," I said, scrambling up.

I perched up there and they hauled me over the crest of the hill with no trouble. Unfortunately, the thing built up so much speed on the downside they couldn't keep hold of the guide ropes, and I whizzed off solo. There was no brake pedal that I could see, so I figured all I could do was keep the clanking heap on the road. Which I did, in spite of the three guys running and shouting on my tail, which might have distracted some people. I careened through the traffic light—green, thank goodness—onto Valley View and sailed past my mother, who was apparently heading home. I couldn't wave because I needed both hands on the wheel, but I grinned.

"A month! I didn't like Camp Blue Ridge last year for two weeks! I'm too old for camp. I'm not going."

"Sarah, you've given us no choice. You had a chance to prove that you're old enough to amuse yourself, and you failed. You have a piano to play, a bicycle to ride, a closet full of art supplies, yet you sat around for weeks whining that you had nothing to do."

"That's not why you're shipping me off. It's the hotrod thing. I know it! This is punishment for that."

She cocked her hand back like she was going to slap me, but I darted around the dining room table. She just stood there glowering at me. "Lower your voice," she snapped. "I'll not discuss this further. You should be grateful we can afford to send you to a lovely camp."

I headed for my room with her still talking. "We'll all come up on your birthday. We'll take you to Blair House for the day."

Whoopee, checked out of prison for my thirteenth birthday. It was so like Mother to give you a life sentence and tell you how lucky you were. What could I do? I knew at that instant that I'd be going, just as sure as a person knows when his tooth hurts like hell he'll be going to the dentist.

"Sarah, stop dawdling. What are you doing in there? If we don't leave this instant you'll miss the camp bus."

"Mother," I called through the bathroom door, "I've got . . . um. . . . I've got a problem." I opened the door; she was standing in the hall with her hands on her hips.

"Sarah."

"But, Mother." I held up a tissue with bright red on it.

She stared at it, her jaw set. From her expression, I thought she was going to slap me, but she just took a huge breath and then let it out. "Sarah, as usual, your timing is perfect. Oh so perfect. We need to leave right now."

"But—"

"Isn't this exciting?" she asked the wall.

"Mother, I can't help it. I'm sorry."

She planted both hands on my shoulders, moved me aside, and came in. She closed the bathroom door with both of us in there and started pulling things out of the closet, things I would need to deal with this problem, the one I'd been thinking about all year. She put them on the counter and walked out, pulling the door shut behind her.

"I feel sort of sick," I said softly.

With that she flung the door back open and it banged against the wall. "You're simply excited about camp. *This* would not cause an upset stomach. Now, we'll be waiting in the car."

Her face was hot pink like the flowers in my bedroom wallpaper, yet she said this in the sweetest voice, then closed the door gently.

I looked at the slingshot contraption and the thick cottony pad she'd taken from the closet, and tried to decide what to do with them. I pulled the stretchy thing over my head and pulled my arms through; it kept snapping at me as I wriggled it down to my waist. I couldn't figure out how to attach the pad to it so I just stuffed it in my pants, yanked up my shorts, and hurried out to the car. It felt like a washcloth folded up and stuck between my legs. It was hard to walk, and I wondered how I'd put up with this for days—or however long it went on.

The camp bus left from North Avenue Presbyterian Church, which was halfway downtown, and Saturday traffic was heavy. By the time we got there girls were already climbing up into the bus. I still felt sick, and Chris and Annie tickling and elbowing each other all the way hadn't made matters easier. Not to mention that my feelings were hurt by Ben, who was too busy to see me off.

"There's Laurie Riley," I hollered.

"Sarah, please," Mother said.

"Oh, I didn't think anybody I knew was going back this year. Hurry, Daddy, I wanna sit with Laurie!"

I managed to catch up with Laurie. She seemed relieved to see a familiar face too. Then, bam, we were being herded onto the bus. I had only a minute to hug Daddy. He slipped me a tight roll of green paper money and whispered, "I love you, sweetie" in my ear. I wondered if he knew what had happened to me that day, if Mother had told him. Mother didn't touch me.

"I put extra supplies in here for you," she said, and stuck my tan duffle bag in my hand. "Behave yourself and do exactly as the counselors tell you. Don't go in that lake unsupervised. And be careful if you sign up for archery. You know Brooks Daniels had his eye put out over at . . ."

I tuned her out. It was so like Mother to tell you on the one hand how privileged you were to go to a camp with horseback riding and swimming and canoeing, not to mention arts and crafts, and so on. But then she'd scare you to death predicting all the atrocious things that could happen to you. You went off a ball of nerves, terrified to set a toe outside your cabin. Which was just as well because, according to her, bugs were going to eat you alive.

There was a roar in our bus all the way to Black Mountain, North Carolina. The girls acted like they'd never been anywhere in

their lives. I'd been to Girl Scout camp at ten and eleven, and Camp
Blue Ridge for snobs last summer; this was no big deal. Laurie and I
played cards on top of her train case until it was time to stop for
dinner. While everyone was unloading, Laurie combed her hair
three times.

"What are you primping for? We're out in the middle of
nowhere."

"You never know, a Y-Camp bus might stop here too," she said,
tossing her honey-blond hair and giggling.

"What would Roy say?"

She ignored my reference to her so-called boyfriend, the high
school boy she'd had a crush on all year. His green eyes and long
eyelashes were all she had talked about.

After dinner, as we rocked along through open fields and
watched the sun set outside our window, Laurie gave me pointers on
my new condition. She knew all about it because she'd "fallen off the
roof" at ten.

"Why do they call it 'falling off the roof'?"

"I have no idea," she said. "I think it's a secret code so boys won't
know what we're talking about. It's dumb; it's as stupid as calling it
'your friend.'"

"How long am I going to feel this awful?"

"Just today," she told me authoritatively.

She instructed me to prop my feet up on the back of the seat in
front of me and hold my duffle on my lap. The pressure did help, but
I felt odd, like my head was full of sand. I had indigestion, too, which
I hardly ever get.

Laurie was right. I did feel better the next day, but I had to keep
wearing the Chinese torture belt and washcloth for six days. It
pitched a grizzly black cloud over outdoor activities such as swim-

ming. Since I had to sit out, it was obvious to all the older girls and counselors what was going on with me. That was humiliating in a way, since this seems like a pretty personal thing. The younger girls who'd been told about menstruating also figured it out and looked at me like "lucky Sarah." I felt embarrassed and special at the same time.

Why, oh why, had I looked forward to this happening? That Tinkerbelle film they showed us at scouts was full of lies. Harp music was playing in it and this adorable blond girl who got "her friend" looked so happy and cute. This was not how it worked for me. It was a pain hiking and riding horseback with a big cotton wad in my drawers.

"My cousin calls 'em Mickey Mouse mattresses," Laurie said, and we laughed, but it really wasn't funny.

The whole camp thing seemed ridiculous to me, childish. I didn't want to be there, and it wasn't fair that everyone else in my family was at home enjoying the summer and spending time with Ben. A part of me wanted to break every camp rule and get kicked out, and believe me I could have done it, snap, just like that. But I didn't have the energy. I felt sleepy and headachy almost daily, so I slogged around and went through the camp routine like I was told. I also crossed off the days on my pocket calendar to July 27—my thirteenth birthday—like a jailbird marking time. My family was coming to spring me that day.

For some reason I wasn't happy to see them when they came. From the moment they arrived in the morning to sign out Laurie and me, all I could think about was them leaving to go back to Atlanta. The day wasn't planned for my enjoyment anyway. Blair

House in Asheville was Mother's choice, not mine, and aside from the homemade chocolate cake Jesse Blair surprised me with after lunch, my birthday faded into the background. And my present, a gold and ruby birth stone ring, had to be whisked back to Atlanta. Mother said it wouldn't be "wise" to have it at camp.

After lunch, Chris and Annie trotted off with cane poles to fish in the pond. Ben sat by the pool with Laurie and me, but with him reading and Laurie chattering about hairstyles and makeup, conversation with Ben was limited. I wondered if we'd ever get to talk before he left for college.

I needed to talk to Ben. I'd never gotten to tell him about something weird I saw just before I left for camp. One morning I caught Mother pawing through the bathroom hamper. She pulled out one of Ben's shirts and examined it—especially the collar. It was the one he'd worn the night before on his date with Connie. What was she searching for? I didn't know but I wanted to ask Ben what he thought she'd been up to.

Hugging them good-bye and watching them pull out through the twisted-tree-limb gate at camp felt as awful as I had known it would. And later, after lights out, when the two wild girls in my cabin from Raleigh suggested we sneak out and shoot off fireworks they'd smuggled in, I went along. Trouble is, *they* didn't get caught. It was me Mrs. Hutchins recognized high-tailing it after we blew up a cherry bomb under her window. Mrs. Hutchins owned the camp. For disturbing her rest and raising her blood pressure, I got latrine-cleaning duty.

Mother's dire predictions about my health at camp came true, of course. I was constipated the whole time and forgot to use the little chewable peppermint tablets she'd packed. I had to go to the infirmary one night my stomach hurt so bad, but the nurse fixed that—

an ordeal I never want to relive. I took all the aspirin in Mother's "emergency kit," but didn't need the poison ivy salve. I've never had poison ivy and I didn't get it this time either. What I did get was some vile, itchy rash on my chest. No one could figure out what it was, not even the town doctor, who dropped by to look at it. Mrs. Hutchins decided I could stick it out for five more days.

"Sarah, honey," she said, "dab a little calamine lotion on that rash every night; it will take the itch out."

Which it did not. I clawed so hard in my sleep that Mother had to take me to a skin doctor on my first day back in Atlanta.

CHAPTER 3

Soon after I got home from camp, Ben left for college. He was going to Vanderbilt University in Nashville; "Vandy," Mother called it. I felt hollow after dinner every night, even after I'd eaten. I couldn't figure out what to do with after-dinner time since I wasn't going to his room to discuss whatever Mother had screamed about at the table. But we weren't fighting at mealtime anymore. Mother's mind seemed to be somewhere else. It was as if Chris, Annie, Daddy, and I were ghosts floating around her.

After school, we would come home to find her either locked in the study reading and underlining in books, or writing in spiral-bound notebooks. Or she'd dash in from the library with an armload of thick books. She announced that she was going to do everything Ben was doing at Vandy—read what his professors assigned and write the papers he had to write. She phoned Ben every day to find out about reading lists and course requirements.

"I want to support Ben in what he's doing. When he comes home at Thanksgiving I'll be able to discuss his work with him."

Mother's plan was for Ben to major in English. "She's convinced I'm going to be the next William Faulkner," he said one night before he left. "Ha!"

We were in his room and I was peeling skin off his back. He had gone to Wakulla Springs, Florida, for a week with Connie and her family and had broiled himself on the beach.

"It's itching like crazy," he said. "Scratch it, slave!" Then he threw himself down on the bed.

I scrunched on the edge beside him and started picking at the bubbles in the flaky waxed paper that used to be skin. "Ewww, this is gross!"

"Scratch!"

"Ben, your whole back is coming off," I shrieked, and I carefully lifted the skin from his back in one big sheet; it rolled up like a window shade and crackled at the edges.

Who knows how Mother convinced Ben to go to Vandy. Being a writer was *her* dream. I saw it in her old high school yearbook, which I came across in the attic. Each girl in the senior class had written under her picture what she thought she'd be doing in ten years. Under a lanky girl who looked not one whit like my mother was printed *Catherine Atwater, Foreign Correspondent for the* New York Times, *Paris, France.*

Ben didn't plan to be a writer. When he was a junior, he came home with catalogs from colleges where you could learn to be an architect, but Mother chucked them in the kitchen trash, laughing like a loon.

Ben didn't come home for Thanksgiving. He called Daddy at work the week before and told him. I guess he didn't have the guts to tell Mother. He'd been invited to spend the holiday with his roommate's family in Highlands, North Carolina. Some other guys from his dormitory were going too. The night Daddy popped the news, my mother slammed the hall door so hard that one of the Audubon birds flew off the wall. The next day, a spidery crack appeared in the ceiling.

It's not that I minded Ben getting a chance to have fun in the mountains, but I missed him. I had some letters on tissuey blue paper he'd sent me, so I went in and dug them out of my underwear drawer. I'd numbered each one, so I was able to read them in order. When I was reading the one about all the stuff we'd do at Thanksgiving, the hi-fi started blaring in Ben's room. I crept down the hall, gently turned the knob on his door, and opened it about an inch. Mother was sitting at Ben's desk staring out the window. She had one of his favorite records playing as loud as it would go. "Oh the shark, babe, has such teeth, dear, and he shows them pearly white . . ."

I didn't breathe, but my mother has radar. She whirled around and bellowed, "Get out! Now!"

We didn't have Thanksgiving dinner. Mother said there would be no Thanksgiving since Ben had ruined everything. She made pork chops, green beans, and apple rings like it was an ordinary day. We couldn't turn on the television because she went right to bed after we ate—at three in the afternoon.

She moped around with a sour expression all weekend, but on Monday she was a wild woman. Suddenly she'd realized it was time to plan for Annie's tenth birthday, and leaped into action. The lace tablecloth appeared, Etha Mae polished the silver, and Mother arranged a centerpiece for the dining room table with rust-colored mums and greenery from our yard. Annie's birthday was really December 22, but we celebrated it on December 1.

"Ann's birthday was always eclipsed by Christmas, so we simply changed it," Mother tells people. "I only wish Mother Nature had seen fit to change it. Being in the hospital at Christmas was inconvenient."

Annie had a skating party at the Rollerdrome, and then her

friend Beth spent the night. Etha Mae stayed late to help, although Mother insisted on frying the chicken—Annie's favorite. Southern fried chicken, and rice with giblet gravy. I don't remember what the vegetable was but I know we had one. Mother insisted on serving balanced meals— a meat, a starch, and a vegetable—birthday or no birthday.

Annie wanted a coconut cake. "Why couldn't she request something simple?" Mother asked Daddy, not waiting for an answer. "I'll never find fresh coconut. On the other hand, why would I even consider baking a coconut cake when Mrs. Friedman makes the best cakes in Atlanta?"

On Saturday afternoon while Daddy was overseeing the kids at the roller rink, Mother drove to Friedman's Bakery on the other side of town to pick up Annie's specially ordered cake. We heard about this inconvenience so many times I think it would have been easier on us if she had just gone ahead and "toiled in the hot kitchen" all day. Or we could have all loaded up and gone to Florida and scaled coconut trees for really fresh fruit; then she could have worked for weeks cracking them open and hand-shredding the coconut meat with a dull knife. I can imagine her telling her friend Amelia how easy it was, really.

Chris tooted his little party horn a few times during the birthday dinner and got the rattlesnake look from Mother, but we all pulled out our best manners that night. Annie didn't wolf her food, Chris didn't tilt back in his chair, and I didn't talk with my mouth full. Mother made polite conversation with Beth and chattered about the Christmas festivities already going on in Atlanta. I thought about the lighting of the giant tree on top of Rich's department store, which we didn't get to see on Thanksgiving because Mother had x'd Thanksgiving off the Claiborne family calendar.

"We haven't driven through Sherwood Forest yet to see the decorations," Daddy said.

Mother shot him the stupidest-person-walking-the-earth look, the same one I got several times a day. "Edward, when would we have had time?" She usually called him Ed, but she used "Edward" whenever she gave him the stupid-you look.

Daddy smiled and nodded. "I know, darling, we have been busy."

"More chicken, Beth?" Mother purred.

After dinner she dimmed the lights and tapped on the swinging door to the kitchen to cue Etha Mae to bring in the cake. It was a huge round cake, four layers, and ablaze with eleven fat candles, one for each of Annie's years and one "to grow on." We all sang "Happy Birthday," Mother the loudest. Annie sucked in a big breath and whooshed out the candles in one blow. Unfortunately, the fresh coconut on top was loose and Annie's gale-force huff shot it all over the table and into the mums.

Every head at the table turned toward my mother during about thirty seconds of stunned silence. Her lips were pursed, but other than turning a purplish color her face was expressionless. She rose, stepped away from the table, and then walked slowly out of the room. Daddy followed her, his brow knit the way it did when he was balancing his check book. The rest of us stared in amazement as the coconut shreds dropped one by one off Mother's beautiful floral creation.

Amelia, this is Catherine. Yes, Etha Mae said you called. I've been trying to reach you. Well, everything's fine, just terribly busy with Thanksgiving, you know, and Annie's birthday, and Christmas.

I loved to eavesdrop on Mother's phone chats with Amelia

Martin—usually gushing about her charming, perfect family. Talk about fiction being presented as fact.

What? No, Ben wasn't here. He had a fabulous opportunity to go to a house party in Highlands. I said, "Ben, we'll regret not having you with us, but you simply cannot pass up an invitation like this!"

Yes, it's magnificent up there. Edward and I honeymooned in Cashiers, you know. At High Hampton, just down the mountain from Highlands.

No, of course not. I didn't want Ben to miss a chance to drink up all that beauty—and relax. He's been burning the midnight oil over those books. He was hesitant about going, but I said, "Christmas is coming, Ben, and you'll be home for three weeks. Now, don't be silly!"

CHAPTER 4

The day school let out for Christmas holidays Wendy and I got a ride to the library. Her mother was at the dentist and mine was at her garden club's Christmas party. We were to wait there until Daddy could get us on his way home from work.

"Lunch was gagacious today," Wendy said. Wendy has a personality to match her red hair and when she can't think of a real word to express her feelings she makes one up. "Didn't you hate it?"

We were in the library bathroom, where I was tapping on some lipstick. Persian Melon. Someone had left it in the girls' locker room at school.

"How could anyone hate turkey?" I asked, kissing a piece of toilet paper so most of the color was gone. I'd have to wipe it off anyway before I went home.

"Let's go down to Roscoe's for onion rings," Wendy said, ignoring my question. "We can get somethin' to eat and be back before your father gets here!"

I turned from the mirror and looked at her. Her Coke-bottle-green eyes were popping out of her freckled face at the thought of breaking a rule. She loved greasy French fries and onion rings, but her mother wouldn't let her eat them.

"Ben calls Roscoe's Ptomaine Tavern," I said, zipping the lipstick tube back in my book satchel. I thought her plan was brilliant but I wanted to tease her a little.

"What's 'ptomaine'?"

"Food poisoning, dummy. Let's go!"

I don't know if it was the cafeteria turkey or Roscoe's hamburger, but I regretted having ever eaten anything in my life about two o'clock that morning. The bed rocked, my head throbbed, and although I swallowed and swallowed, the lump lodged in my throat insisted on moving up. I careened down the hall to the bathroom.

"What in the world, Sarah?"

Mother clicked on the overhead light. I was crouched in front of the toilet, clinging to the seat. The room was spinning, and I was too sick to answer. Mother came closer and put her hand on my forehead. "You're clammy," she said, reaching for a washcloth.

When I had finally stopped throwing up, I eased back and sat on my heels. Mother had waited me out, perched on the clothes hamper. She got up and ran water over the cloth and squeezed it, leaned over and dabbed at my mouth. She rinsed the cloth, wrung it out again, and then applied it to my forehead.

I wanted to stay right there, but Mother helped me back to my bed, smoothed the covers around me, and placed the cool washcloth on my head. She left the room just for a minute, but when she came back I was already drifting off.

"I'm putting a bell here on your bedside table, honey," she said. "If you feel sick again, just ring it. I'm going back to bed, but I'll be sleeping with my ears open."

Then she kneeled down and kissed my cheek.

My temperature hovered around 103 degrees the next day. I knew I was dying of ptomaine poisoning but would take that knowledge to my grave before confessing to Mother about Roscoe's.

"I think it's flu," she told Daddy when he looked in on us. "I'm calling William."

"Urghh . . ." was all I could say. Their good friend William Timberlake, my pediatrician, would want her to bring me into his office, and I barely had energy to breathe.

Who knows what Dr. T's nurse told Mother when she phoned but I didn't have to get up, and Mother spent the day shuttling back and forth between the ice crusher in the kitchen and my bedside. "Let's get a little of this in you," she said, spooning ice chips in my mouth. I would let them melt on my tongue, struggle to swallow, then go back to sleep.

On the second day my stomach had stopped hurting but my legs felt like boards and my back ached and cramped. It was as if a grizzly bear were gripping my spine. Squeeze, release. Squeeze, release. Mother was impatient with my refusals of food or drink. All day I turned down her offers: saltine crackers, chicken bouillon, Jell-O. Coca-Cola on crushed ice was all I could manage.

The next day I heard her leave the house. Etha Mae came in and asked if I'd like some scrambled eggs.

"I'll try," I croaked, my voice scratchy from not saying anything yet that morning. I could hear Etha Mae mumbling "Lawd, have mercy" as she plodded down the hall to the kitchen.

When Mother got back from her errands and found me propped up in bed eating Etha Mae's eggs, she drew in a deep breath, let it out in a huge huff, and walked away. I didn't see her for the rest of the day. Etha Mae tended to me, and by 4:30 when she left to catch the maid's bus, I had managed a bowl of chicken noodle soup and a few wheat thins. But I was still weak and couldn't even flip through a movie magazine. Instead I lay there flat on my back staring at the ceiling and trying to identify footsteps in our house. Chris's were noisy, thumpy, and quick. Annie's were muffled and slow. She always tiptoed. Most of the time you didn't even know she was in the house. Daddy's were easy to recognize since he wore leather shoes, size 12. A man's step in large, hard-soled shoes is heavy. I can't tell you about Mother's though. You never heard her coming. She would just all of a sudden be there. No warning. Like last summer.

I had a Spring cigarette I'd gotten from Judy Burgess. I thought Mother had left, gone to the Salon of Beauty to get her hair done. I sat down at my vanity, lit up, and tilted my head back to look like a movie star, letting the smoke spiral up out of my loose lips. I was Maggie the Cat in my slip. Well, okay, Maggie didn't wear a training bra. Anyway, I never heard one step and there she was, opening my door, staring at me in horror. She pounced, grabbed my knees and squeezed hard. Then she caught my wrist with one hand and removed the cigarette with the other. "Ooooo. Ooooo." She stood there holding that cigarette, looking at me with the rattlesnake eyes, saying "ooooo" over and over.

"Sarah Atwater Claiborne," she said, "I want to burn you with this cigarette." She held it an inch from my kneecap for a second, then spun around and marched out of the room. I could hear her high-heel patent leather pumps clicking down the hall as she left. But you could never hear her when she was coming to you. It was always, always a surprise.

Mother brought me a dinner tray and suggested I eat in the armchair that she referred to as my "reading chair."

"You'll digest better if you eat sitting up."

She was right. I ate a good bit of the mashed potatoes and the tops of the asparagus. But the roast beef made me think of Roscoe's hamburger. I cut off a few bites, folded them in my napkin, and tucked the bundle in my bathrobe pocket so I could flush it later. Annie came in and took my tray and I crawled back into bed. Dishes were clattering out in the kitchen. Soon Mother appeared, holding a thin blue book. "I had to search all over Atlanta to find this today, but I knew you'd enjoy it."

She handed me the book. *A Child's Christmas in Wales* by Dylan Thomas.

"What's it about?"

"It's not long. Would you like me to read it to you?"

She'd lost her mind. I was thirteen; I could read. But she looked so hopeful and I was too tired to argue. "Okay," I said, and put down the article I was reading about Natalie Wood. The story would probably be sappy, but I would pretend to listen.

"'One Christmas was so much like another in those years around the sea-town corner now and out of all sound except the distant speaking of the voices I sometimes hear a moment before sleep, that I can never remember whether it snowed for six days and six nights when I was twelve or whether it snowed for twelve days and twelve nights when I was six . . .'"

It was hard to concentrate on the story. I closed my eyes and tried to picture the two boys waiting to pelt neighborhood cats with snowballs. But I drifted off during something about church bells. "'And they rang their tidings over the bandaged town, over the frozen foam of the powder and ice-cream hills . . .'"

Probably I dreamed about ice-cream sundaes. Mother tells people, "Sarah doesn't have a sweet tooth; she has thirty-two sweet teeth."

When something jiggled my bed, I woke up with a start. Mother was still in my chair. She had closed the book and was smiling. Daddy was stretched out on my other twin bed and he winked at me.

Chris and Annie were sprawled on the floor at the foot of my bed. Chris was kicking the footboard. Annie stood up, stretched, and leaped on me.

"Wasn't that a neat story?" she asked and poked my ribs.

"What's going on here? How come everybody's in my room?"

They laughed at me—Mother too.

When I was sick I had time to think, and I realized how peaceful things had been during those days. Mother seemed enthusiastic about Christmas and Ben coming home. Daddy whistled a good bit, and Chris lowered himself to enter the sick room and ask how I felt. Unfortunately, he kept kicking the bed and I demanded that he leave. Even Annie sat with me one afternoon and chattered about her Christmas wish list. Annie seemed like someone from another planet to me. She was into little girlie things like tea sets and paper dolls; at her age all I wanted to do was climb trees and build forts with the boys.

Anyway, I decided to try acting a little more like Miss Priss Annie when I arose from my sick bed; I'd be the model older daughter. I suppose I was as determined as Mother to make this a story-book Christmas, make everything just right for Ben's homecoming. I hadn't seen him since August and couldn't wait for him to come home.

Mother must have studied the Cleaver family on TV for tips on having the perfect American Christmas because she always turned our museum home into a yuletide wonderland. This year, she personally swagged evergreen garland on the wrought iron railings at the front stoop. Under her eagle eye, Daddy hung the elegant Frazier fir wreath with pine cones and nuts on the front door. Deep red hand-dipped candles replaced the ivory ones in the gold sconces in the living room. Limoges candy dishes were filled with individually wrapped Christmas candies.

"Aww—what is this stuff?" Chris howled, spitting a piece in his hand.

"I don't know, Chris, she ordered 'em. They're made in England. Probably back in Shakespeare's day."

"Who's Shake-peer?"

"Chris, go flush that thing and wash your hands."

The living room furniture had to be totally rearranged so the tree could be centered in front of the bay window. Decorating the tree, picked out by Daddy from the lot at Frank's Curb Market, was the only thing "the kids" were ever involved in. Ben usually played Christmas carols on the piano while Chris and Annie bickered about where to hang ornaments—hideous cardboard and tin-can things they made at school—while I oversaw placement of the beautiful sparkly breakable ones.

This year, with Ben off at college, I couldn't get interested. I stretched out on the sofa to watch my little brother and sister sling a bunch of ornaments on the right side of the tree. It seemed to me it was so heavy on that one side that it might collapse, but I held my tongue. June Cleaver obviously visited that night while we slept, as our tree was a sight to behold the next morning—every antique ornament and hand-blown ball hung at the front, and every kid-made atrocity magically relocated toward the back. The Claiborne tree was always good enough for the cover of the Sunday magazine section, should a roving photographer from the *Atlanta Constitution* happen by.

The day before Ben was to come home, she sat us down and gave us our instructions. Her museum was ready and she wanted to make sure we were too. "Now, children, your brother has been working very hard for the last four months. We know college work is challenging, especially at a fine university like Vanderbilt. Even for someone as bright as your brother. Now, listen to me." She paused and pointed at each of us, one at a time. "You are not, I repeat, not to pester Ben."

Silence.

"Is that clear?"

Silence.

"And no racing around the house. We're going to have a lovely, relaxing Christmas. Is that understood?"

"We should never have allowed Ben to ride home with that girl, whoever she is. There's ice and snow on the—who is Sandra Levin?—they could slide off and end up in a ditch and freeze to death.

"Annie, please get your brother's old class directory. Let's try to determine where this Sandra person lives.

"I should have insisted he take the train. Oh, I hope Ben hasn't gotten a horrible cold. He wasn't prepared for a snowstorm up there *before* Christmas. Nothing but that skimpy windbreaker.

"Ed, why don't you and Annie run up to the Rexall and pick up some Vick's and aspirin. We're out of aspirin. I know Ben's going to have chest congestion.

"Sarah, have you done something about your room? Your records were strewn all over the floor. Instead of roaming the house like a caged animal you might make yourself useful.

"Has anyone found that person . . . that Sandra's phone number? I'm calling that girl's mother. What was the woman thinking of? No daughter of mine would be driving an automobile on frozen highways.

"Edward, just unplug the tree. I'm going to lie down. It's plain to see there's not going to be a Christmas this year. Noop. No Christmas for the Claibornes."

CHAPTER 5

*I*t was almost dark when Ben got home. He and Sandra, a senior at Vanderbilt, had gotten a late start.

"I went very slowly," she told Daddy when he and I went out to see if we could help carry in Ben's things.

"How were the roads?" Daddy asked.

"Slick at first, but not so bad once we got out of Nashville," Ben said.

Sandra was quiet and kind of shy. She wouldn't come in, but asked us to call her mother to say she'd be home soon.

"Good luck, Ben," she said as she climbed back in her gray Chevy. Odd thing to say. Why not, "Merry Christmas" or "I'll see you in January"?

"Hey, Ben," I said. "Thanks for sending me *Streetcar Named Desire*. I finished it about two minutes ago."

"That's good," Ben said, his voice heavy. I guess he was tired. I had thought he'd be anxious to talk to me about the story.

Inside, Chris and Annie were all over Ben. Annie made him hot chocolate, and Chris brought in his best baseball cards—not the whole box—to show him. Daddy built a fire and we sat around asking Ben questions. We stared at him too; it had been a long time since we saw him. He looked different. He had a stubbly beard like he hadn't shaved for a week.

"If you grew a mustache, you'd have a hole right there," Annie told him, touching a blank space over his lip where there was no blond stubble. It was like he'd shaved a tiny path through it.

We were all acting formal, like he was a long-lost prince come back to the palace. Only the queen wasn't around.

"Where's Mother?" Ben asked, glancing at me.

"Napping, I guess." I rolled my eyes so he would know she was in one of her tailspins.

The queen never emerged from her chamber. Daddy and Ben fixed tomato soup and grilled cheese sandwiches for us, then Ben took off in Daddy's car to see Connie. Chris and Annie went to their rooms. Daddy poked at the fire, paced, jingled his pocket change. There was nothing on television but old Christmas movies. I had to get out of there, so I took to the attic with my new *Photoplay*. I read and daydreamed, then dozed off. When someone touched my arm, I jerked, startled.

"Ben! Oh my gosh. What time . . . ?" I rubbed my arm where a watch would be if I wore one.

"Midnight. I got in from Connie's and saw the light in your room, but you weren't there."

I yawned and stretched.

"Was there a blow-up?" he asked.

"No. Mother never came out . . . I don't think."

He frowned.

"It's so weird. She's been getting ready for you to come home for weeks. Then you get here and she never even says hello."

"Look, Sally, I've got to tell you something right now so you can be prepared." Ben pulled an old maple rocker out of the corner and sat in it at the foot of the cot. I propped up on my elbows so I could see him. "While I'm home I'm going to tell Mother something she's not going to want to hear."

"What?"

"I hate Vanderbilt; I'm not staying there. I'll go back after Christmas and finish out the semester; after that, I'm not sure what I'll do."

"What's the matter with Vandy?"

Ben rubbed his eyes and stared at the floor.

"You miss me and Chris and Annie, don't you? And Connie. I'll bet you really miss Connie. And your room, and—"

"It's Vanderbilt. I'm bored to death. I'm not interested in any of my classes. I have no friends."

"You don't have any friends?"

"I'm in a dorm with all these football players. I mean, they're all right, but . . . I don't know. I sleep all the time. It's bleak up there."

"But how 'bout your roommate? You spent Thanksgiving with him."

"No, I didn't." I started to speak but he interrupted. "Look, Sarah, there's no reason to talk about this anymore. I just wanted to warn you. I'm sure she'll flip her lid."

My stomach was squeezing. I had a thousand questions. How could he not come home at Thanksgiving? Where was he? Did he know what happened here?

He stood up to leave. "Oh, Ben, I loved *Streetcar*. Wasn't it so good? That Stanley was gross, always screaming at Stella."

He sat back down and stared out the window into the darkness.

"Ben, can I ask you something?"

"Sarah, I said I didn't want to—"

"No, Ben, about the play. Who was the man at the end who came for Blanche?"

He thought for a minute. "He was a doctor."

"Oh. Well, who was the woman with him?"

"A nurse, I guess."

"Oh."

"Sally, Blanche was nuts. They were taking her away to a hospital."

"You thought she was crazy? Oh, I don't think so."

"She lived in a dream world. She wanted things a certain way, and they weren't. She couldn't face it, you know? Remember how she hated bare light bulbs?"

I didn't.

"Blanche couldn't face reality, Sarah. The bare truth."

Knowing what Ben was going to tell Mother, I couldn't sleep. I lay in bed, my teeth chattering, wondering how I could avert a disaster. Dim light was leaking in through the blinds when I decided that it wouldn't be so bad. Mother would convince Ben to stay at Vanderbilt, or she'd let him study architecture at Tech, right here in Atlanta.

It seemed like I'd been in bed for only a few hours when the sun came up.

"Come on, Sarah, get up," Annie said, tugging my arm. "Let's go in there or they're never going to get up!"

"Unnh."

"Come on! I've already peeked and my bike's there!"

For the first time in my life I wasn't excited about Christmas morning. There'd be nothing great under the tree for me because I wanted clothes; no way my parents would try to buy me clothes. I'm picky and hard to fit. Too tall, and too skinny. Skirts are always too short and stand out at the waist. Forget dresses. I had a list of records I wanted, but I never gave it to them.

Chris came in and leaped on the end of my bed. "Time to get up. Santy Claus came!" He was practically screaming.

"Oh, OK. Go get Ben up. I'm coming."

The Christmas morning scene was like a play I'd already been to. The little corner where my "Santa Claus" surprises were arranged was skimpy, just as I'd expected. Once I'd thumbed through the few things, I put them back exactly the way Mother had arranged them. (Mother was Santa Claus at our house; I'm sure even Chris knew that.) There was a gift certificate for me to buy some clothes at Rich's; a flannel bathrobe, which I put on, then took off because the sleeves were too short; a couple of 45s I didn't much want; a year's subscription to *Teen* magazine, which I liked, but it was just a card promising that the magazine would start coming in January, so it wasn't actually there for me to look at; some slipper socks; and a silver charm for my charm bracelet—some kind of bird.

As I went through my pile, Chris kept interrupting to show off his loot: a midnight blue airplane model, vials of chemicals from the Mr. Wizard set, a leather baseball glove for his right hand—Chris is left-handed. Annie bounced around like a human pogo stick because she got the 26-inch bicycle she wanted. I stared at her, amazed. Quiet Annie, whose favorite role was Miss Disappear-into-the-woodwork, bouncing. Sometimes she got enthusiastic about food, but nothing like this. Today she was as perky as Gidget, dressed and ready to haul the bike out the front door before our parents made it to the living room.

"We'd better not take one single thing out of this room before the Clauses get here, Annie. You know what I mean."

"Sarah, are you in a bad mood today?"

"No, Annie, I'm not in a bad mood. I just want to get this over with so I can go over to Wendy's."

Then the Clauses came in. "Merry Christmas!" Mother sang out in the exaggerated happy tone she uses on Christmas mornings. "Where's Ben?"

I decided right then to click out of being Sarah and become a visitor in the Claiborne house. An observer. It was too phony to be a part of, going through every step we always went through. Maybe every American family does this, I thought. The kids show Mom and Dad what Santa brought in the night, and Mom and Dad pretend to be surprised.

We took turns opening gifts under the tree, while Mother wrote down each item so we could write thank-you notes to everybody— aunts, uncles, cousins, my grandmother in Savannah.

Ben and I had always put off writing the notes until after New Year's, even though it would have been easier to go ahead and do it that day because Mother hounded us every minute until they were written and handed to her to mail.

The next step was to have a healthy, hot breakfast because we'd only nibbled on sweet rolls and sipped orange juice during the unwrapping step. But it didn't happen that way this year. Ben opened our parents' gift, a heavy winter coat, brown tweed. A really nice coat from Buckhead Men's Shop.

"Ben, you don't look pleased with the coat," Mother said the minute he opened the box. "We thought you'd be thrilled. Would you rather have had the charcoal?"

"I—"

"I combed Atlanta for that coat."

"I—"

"There was nothing you'd have wanted at Rich's or Davison's. I can tell you that. Now, slip it on, let's see."

She stood up and took the coat from him. "Here." She whipped it up and held it like a matador holds the cape for the bull.

Ben went along with her, but once he had it on he looked right at her and said, "Mother, I think it's going to be too heavy."

"What?"

"I've decided to drop out of Vanderbilt at the end of the semester. I won't be needing a coat this heavy."

I casually looked over to observe Mother's face, as any theatergoer would do. What would the next line be? Since I was not a character in the family play that day, I was totally calm, numb actually, and able to pay attention. Daddy was out in the kitchen getting more juice, and Annie and Chris were fiddling with their presents. Ben and I were the only ones to witness her reaction. Her face froze into a white mask with two small brown circles for eyes. Just for a minute it froze solid like the ice on the inside of our freezer. Then it cracked into five or ten pieces, like a puzzle. But, bam, it froze back into a solid, flat face again. Bam, bam, bam. Just like that. Freeze, crack, freeze.

When the last freeze came, it stayed, and she said in a teacher voice, "Children, clear up your things now and take them to your rooms, please. Ben and I are going to talk and we would like not to be interrupted.

"Ed. Edward."

Daddy appeared from the kitchen.

"Ed, would you come in here. Ben would like to talk with you. Sarah, help your brother and sister get their things to their rooms, would you, dear?"

No one said a word, and Chris and Annie and I marched out as fast as we could with towers of boxes teetering in our arms.

I made my bed, dressed, and organized my presents, listening for hollering and door-slamming. But it was quiet. I figured Ben had done a good job of explaining to Mother and Daddy how he felt, just like he'd told me in the attic. I was starving, so I went to the kitchen. Daddy was there making sandwiches since it was too late for breakfast. Mother and Ben were nowhere to be seen. Daddy said Annie and Chris had eaten and were outside playing; he said he would take me to Wendy's. I didn't ask why Ben wasn't driving me as planned. It didn't seem like Christmas in our house anymore. No turkey was being prepared. No jolly Christmas floats were parading across the TV screen.

"Daddy, we never checked to see what was in our stockings."

"I know, honey, I know."

It happened so fast, I can't piece it together in my memory. Ben didn't go back to Vanderbilt. He got on a Greyhound bus to New Orleans two days after Christmas. I went to his room the night before he left to find out why he wasn't going back to take his exams—or get his clothes! He wouldn't answer my questions. He was packing like a robot, grinding back and forth from his dresser to his suitcase. Walk, pick-up, fold, bend.

"Sarah, you're welcome to sit and talk to me, but I don't want to discuss this." He stopped and looked at me. "OK?"

"Did something happen with you and Connie?"

"Sarah!" He raised his voice, and I couldn't stand for Ben to be mad at me, so as much as I wanted to know what had happened, I dropped it. I couldn't understand why Ben had changed so much. It was as if the brother I'd had all my life went off to college and never came back. The brother I had before would have told me every detail. What Mother said and did, what Daddy thought, what Connie's reaction was. And we would've put our heads together and figured out what we could do about it.

The Ben I knew would have also told me why of all places he was going to New Orleans, and what he was going to do there. But since he'd been home he seemed to have forgotten what we used to do. This person posing as my brother didn't know how neat Ben was either. This stranger hardly ever shaved or combed his hair; his clothes looked slept in. I didn't know what to say, so I just sat and watched him.

Mother never came out of her room the next morning while Daddy and Ben loaded Ben's stuff in the car. Daddy asked me and Chris and Annie to ride with them, but we all turned him down. Annie hugged Ben and ran to her room crying. Chris hugged Ben's knees, said his friend Beau was outside waiting, and dashed out the front door. I hugged him fast and stiff. He was a robot so I would be one too.

"I'll write you, Sally," he said and messed up my hair. "You'd better write me back. OK?"

"My name's Sarah," I said, deadpan.

I stood at the bay window in our living room, peered around the Christmas tree, and watched them pull out of our driveway. I thought about going back to Annie's room to see if she was all right, or maybe going out to my chinaberry tree or up to the attic. I didn't know what to do, so I sat down in the chair by our fireplace. I was shivery, and there was a little warmth coming from the fire Daddy had built.

Some gifts were still under the tree. Our present to Mother was propped under there. I hadn't seen her unwrap it. It was a big color picture of Ben and me and Chris and Annie, all four of us standing in front of the pink dogwood in our front yard. Connie took it with Ben's camera last summer, and Ben and I had picked out the frame.

Mother never liked anything anybody gave her. But we thought she'd love this because she was always complaining about not having a good picture of the four of us. Who knows whether she liked it or not. Right then, I wanted to smash the thing with a sledge hammer.

Part Two

I stayed at Belle Reve and tried to hold it together! I'm not meaning this in any reproachful way, but all the burden descended on my shoulders.

Tennessee Williams, *Streetcar Named Desire*

CHAPTER 6

About a month after Ben left, Mother went to the hospital to have a lump removed from her breast. Our house was quiet and still. And empty. I didn't realize how she filled the house until she was out of it. Since Christmas she'd hardly left home except to run to the grocery store or take Etha Mae to the bus stop. She had been busy with her investigation. Chief Detective Claiborne hung on the phone constantly, grilling people about Ben.

"Something happened up there," she said to my father.

"Darlin', I don't think Vanderbilt was the right place for him."

"Listen, my son was traumatized in some way, and I plan to find out why and how and who is responsible. We may need to go up there; if I can't make any more headway with those people than I have this week, we *will* go. They're avoiding me; I know it. It's obvious they're scurrying around in their little ivory towers trying to cover something up."

"Catherine, don't you think—"

"No, Edward, I don't think . . . I *know*. A normal person doesn't go off to college and come home four months later to pack up, move, and totally cut off his family and friends. Not without some precipitating event, something so heinous I don't want to think about it!"

Her crying trailed off and then their bedroom door slammed. I could hear Daddy going in after her. Ben hadn't cut off the whole family; I'd gotten three or four letters from him and Chris and Annie got a picture-postcard with a New Orleans streetcar on it. Ben also said in one of his letters that he had called Daddy a few times at his office. My father never keeps secrets, so Mother had to know she was the only person Ben "cut off."

He didn't have a phone in his apartment, so she couldn't call him. And I imagine she wrote but didn't get answers.

"Well, what's the news from your brother?" she asked me in a fake cheerful voice an hour after his first letter came.

"He's fine."

"That's it, Sarah? He's fine?"

"Well, he is, Mother. He found an apartment. He can see the Mississippi River from his window. And he got a job."

"Oh, really! I can't imagine what kind of job an eighteen-year-old with a high school education could manage. It's such a waste, such a pathetic waste. With all his intelligence . . ."

She raved on about Ben's brilliance and talents, then went on with her frantic telephone calling to solve the mystery. She even called Connie, but didn't find out much. Connie was in the dark like the rest of us.

I had as many questions as Mother did. Why was Ben doing this to her? She worshiped him. But other than telling me he didn't like Vandy, he never explained anything. His letters breezed over the past and into what he was doing, like exploring the French Quarter. He said there were strange people there, and he rambled on about the odd characters he'd seen in the Quarter. The only thing I knew about the French Quarter was what I read in *Streetcar Named Desire*. It sounded like a dirty, gloomy place. But Ben seemed thrilled to be able to watch a man in the laundromat every week who doused his own body with Clorox. Apparently the guy thought Martians were trying to extinguish him with rays, which he believed the Clorox blocked.

Eventually I gave up trying to get answers and just felt lucky to hear from him. I had other problems to deal with—like Phil Patrick wanting to be my boyfriend.

Phil Patrick started calling after we went back to school in January. He sat five seats away from me in chorus. His first call was about an assignment. We were to do exercises to help us breathe with our diaphragm; and he wanted to know how long we were supposed to do them every day. I didn't think anything of it. The second time he called he said he thought I was cute. I didn't know what to say, so I laughed.

"I watch you when we're singing," he said. "You look good from the side. I like how your front teeth do. It's cute."

"My front teeth?"

"Yeah, the top ones."

"What about my top teeth? I don't get it."

"I dunno. It's hard to explain."

"That is so dumb."

"Can you wait for me after class tomorrow?"

I met him after chorus the next day and he walked me to PE and loaned me a book about mind-reading. He wanted to know what I thought about it.

"He's too short for you," Wendy said.

"What do you mean?"

"If you're going to have a boyfriend, he should be at least as tall as you."

"There's no boy in the eighth grade as tall as me, Wendy, in case you hadn't noticed, and he's not my boyfriend."

But Phil Patrick was nice and I liked it when he called. We talked about interesting things: mummies, ghosts, ESP, was there life in outer space.

Mother was annoyed that I tied up the phone; she was waiting for return calls having to do with her investigation.

"Phil's uncle is Rod Serling, the man who writes *The Twilight Zone* stories," I told her one night. She was fixing dinner, and she dropped a pot.

"Really? Does he ever come to visit, dear?"

"I don't know, Mother."

"Well, ask Phil, dear."

She seemed more interested in me at that moment than she had since I was chosen to be a tulip in the May Day program in kindergarten. I forgot to ask Phil if his uncle ever came to their house. And Mother forgot because she went to the hospital to have the lump taken out.

"Mornin', Miss Sarah, Miz Claiborne asked us to come by and do some furniture movin.'"

"She's in the hospital, Moses."

"Yessum, but she asked us to come take care of the movin' before she gets home."

Moses, who works at Daddy's office, pulled a folded paper from his jacket and read it out loud. "Double bed from Mister and Miz Claiborne's room to attic. Twin beds from storage room."

I showed Moses and his brother William in and led them back to my parents' bedroom. "That's the attic," I said as we passed the attic door. "The storage room's out over the garage."

I loved my parents' bed. It had the softest mattress in the house, and I wondered why she'd want to switch it out for old hard-as-rock twin beds. I started to ask Moses to move the big bed into my room, but decided against it. Mother would be home from the hospital the next day, and if she was her usual self, she'd be furious; she'd had special spreads made for my twin beds.

"What's cancer, Daddy?" Annie asked at the dinner table.

"It's a disease, honey."

"Can we catch it?"

"No, sweetheart, and we hope Mother doesn't have cancer anymore. Dr. Long removed the lump, and he thinks she'll be all right. So we were lucky."

"How'd he get that lump out of Mama?" Chris asked, plopping a glob of butter on his potatoes.

"Dr. Long is a surgeon, son. He cut the lump out."

Chris doubled over, clutched his stomach.

"Chris, when you have an operation, you're put to sleep and you don't feel it."

"Oh," Chris said, uncoiling.

No more was said on the topic until Chris finished eating and ran off to his room. Then Daddy told Annie and me that Mother was still hurting and sleeping a lot and that we needed to be quiet around the house when she came home.

What's new, I thought.

He didn't tell us how terrible Mother looked. She wasn't fat before, but she had some padding. At five-foot-ten you'd call her a big person. She also has a strong voice. When she walks into a room, everybody looks at her. Once when she whirled into my school to get something straightened out on my report card, everyone in the office—a big office—buzzed around getting what Mrs. Claiborne needed and doing what Mrs. Claiborne wanted done. The first time Phil Patrick met her he said he felt like he ought to click his heels and salute her.

He wouldn't have said that the day she came home from the operation. She was gray-looking and thin and seemed, I don't know, *scared*. Daddy pulled the car up to the back door and helped her in. She clutched her left arm to her side and held onto Daddy's arm with the other. She mumbled hello to me and Etha Mae in a weak voice as we backed into the kitchen to let them pass.

"Miz Claiborne been through an awful time, Miss Sarah," Etha Mae said, scrubbing a pot she'd had soaking in the sink. "I know she feels real bad about them taking her bosom."

"What?"

"Mr. Claiborne said the cancer spread out." She dried the pot and held it up to inspect it. "So the doctor, he had to take off her whole bosom and even some limp no."

"Some what?"

"These here up under her arm, Miss Sarah."

"Nobody told *me* about this! Daddy said they took out the lump."

I yanked the chair out from under the kitchen table, dropped in it, and crossed my arms over my chest. My breasts had been growing steadily for a year. At first, I hated them and got furious every time I looked in the mirror. Now I didn't think much about them until one of the senior boys ogled them in the hall. I looked down and tried to imagine how I'd feel if there was only one. Etha Mae filed away the shiny pan and came up behind me. She patted me on my shoulder and let out a big breath I felt on my neck.

———•———

"Will she be able to go swimming?" Wendy asked. "Can she wear a bathing suit?"

I was forced to confide in Wendy. Annie was too young. Ben was gone. Daddy was out of the question; he lied to us in the first place, and in the second place it embarrassed me to think about discussing it with him.

"I don't know. I hadn't thought about that."

"Can you tell? When she's wearing clothes, can you tell?"

"Yeah. You can. This woman came to fit her with some rubber thingamajig that goes in her bra."

"Neat."

"No, Wendy, it doesn't look right. It's not the same size as the other one."

"Did you say anything?"

"No."

"Does she talk about it?"

"Nope. She cries. That's all she does. Lie in bed and cry."

Wendy smeared more peanut butter on a pine cone and set it carefully in our row on the kitchen table. Wendy's mom always had her kids involved in some nature project, and today they were creating pine cone feeders to hang out in the trees for the birds. We were doing the peanut butter step and then Wendy's little brother, Joe, was supposed to roll them in wild birdseed.

"How do these hang?" I asked.

"My mom does a string-thing at the top. Or ribbon. What causes cancer?'

"Mother said Daddy flung his fist out in his sleep one night and hit her, and that caused it. In her anyway."

"Really? That could cause a disease?"

"Yep."

"You should ask Mrs. Stafford in Health about that. That doesn't sound right."

I never spoke to Mrs. Stafford; again, it was too embarrassing. Mother wouldn't want a report from me anyway. She had come out of her crying phase and was on the warpath—after me. Suddenly she was furious with me all the time, especially when I talked to Phil. One night we were on the phone and I heard a click, then breathing.

"Hello? I'm on the phone."

Click.

"What was that?" Phil asked.

"I guess someone needs the phone."

"Well, I'll finish telling you about this real quick. Um, anyway, nobody knows how all those gigantic rocks got piled up like that. Humans couldn't have done it. Not in those days. They didn't have cranes."

Click.

"Hello?"

"Sarah?"

"Yes, ma'am?"

"Get off the phone."

Click.

"Phil, I'd better go."

It happened every night. She was trying to break me down, I'm sure, wanting me to just give up talking to Phil.

I complained to Wendy.

"What's she doing now?"

"Trying to drive me crazy. I think she wants me hauled off to Milledgeville."

"Milledgeville?"

"The insane asylum."

"Come on, Sarah."

"She never lets me talk on the phone. Every time I get on she tells me to get off."

"Maybe she wants you to do your homework."

"I don't know. She doesn't explain; she gives orders. I think she's been going through my drawers too."

"Really?"

"Yep. I think she may have found Ben's letters I had hidden in there."

"Is there anything secret in the letters?"

"They're *my* letters. If Ben wanted to write her, he'd write her."

"Well, I've got an idea about your phone calls. At my house we have certain times we can use the phone at night, after we do our homework. Maybe you can set up something like that."

"My mother won't do that."

"Why not?"

"She wouldn't have anything to yell about."

"You're not going with the Patricks tonight, Sarah."

"What?"

"Don't 'what' me!"

"Why not, Mother?"

"I've thought long and hard about this; you're rushing things. You're too young to be going on dates."

"They're not dates. Phil's dad drives us to choir concerts. That's it. And one time I rode my bike to Lenox Square to meet him for a Coke."

"You have no business hanging around Lenox Square. You could get kidnapped."

"What?"

"Don't 'what' me, Sarah Claiborne. *The Atlanta Journal* said child molesters lurk around these new malls."

"OK, I'll go over to Phil's next time. It's no farther than Lenox."

"You certainly will not go over to a boy's house where his parents might not be home. Have you taken leave of your senses?"

"Mother, why—"

"Don't argue, Sarah. The answer is no."

No talking on the phone. No going anywhere with Phil. No having Wendy over because it wasn't "convenient." That meant Mother napped in the afternoon and didn't want to be disturbed. Then my record player was too loud for her and she confiscated a stack of my 45s.

"Where's 'Sea of Love'? And 'Love Me Tender'?"

"I reviewed your records. I listened carefully to all of them, and what I heard on some was startling."

"What? Which one?"

"Don't interrupt me. Several of those records were inappropriate. I've disposed of them."

I never mentioned the rules and searches and seizures to my father until after the incident with Annie. One afternoon I came in from school and she was sitting on a stool in the kitchen, sobbing. Spread out on the counter in front of her were a bag of potato chips, a box of cookies, a jar of peanut butter, and a quart of butter pecan ice cream, open and melting.

"Good grief, Annie. What are you doing?"

She didn't answer, just kept bawling. I stuck the top back on the ice cream and put it in the freezer.

"I only wanted one," Annie said.

"One what?"

"Peanut butter cookie. I was getting it and Mommy came in and said if I wanted to be fat to just go ahead and be fat. She pulled out all this stuff and said I had to sit here and eat every single thing before I could leave the kitchen."

"Annie, go on back to your room."

She started crying again and didn't budge, so I went downstairs where Mae was ironing and asked her to come help. Somehow she talked Annie into going outside.

That night I told Daddy what had happened and how Mother had been picking on me too. He just shook his head and said, "Oh, honey." He ran his hand through his hair and went back to looking at some papers he'd brought home from work. He seemed to be puzzling over something.

For a while after the surgery, Mother wouldn't see friends who came by, or talk to them when they called. She wouldn't speak to my grandmother on the phone either, although I can't blame her there. But now that she had taken on the job of making our lives miserable she'd bounced back. Her first chat with Amelia Martin would've won the "Biggest Liar in the Western World" contest. I could hear only her end of the conversation, of course.

I am feeling better, thank you. And thank you so much for the lovely plant. Such a beautiful deep pink.

On the thirteenth? Oh, I'm not sure, Amelia. I may have garden club that day.

Yes, yes, and now they're busy with their activities and school. Well, I do try to stay involved—helping with homework and what not.

Ben? He's fine. Loving New Orleans!

Hmm? Oh, you know these young people. They don't communicate. And I'll tell you, I blame that Kerouac character. That madman tells them to forget college, experience life.

No, I'm not upset. He's just having a little adventure. You know, we're convinced he's down there writing a novel.

That's right. He just might make us all famous.

Helping us with our homework. That was interesting. Hadn't happened in my lifetime. That night, in fact, when she appeared in my doorway I thought she'd come to try to make good on at least one of her lies.

"May I come in?"

"Yeah."

"*Yes, ma'am.* Does being a teenager bring on amnesia, Sarah? You seem to have blanked out in the manners department."

"Yes, ma'am. I mean, no, ma'am."

What had I done wrong this time? I was stretched out on my bed doing homework on the study board Daddy made for me. She closed the door and sat down on the twin bed opposite me.

"Sarah, I'm concerned about something, and I need you to work with me."

I looked at her.

"Amelia's friend Corinne Brice had the same operation I had—a mastectomy. I went to visit her today because she's been deeply depressed.

"They did the same thing to her they did to me. They took her breast and sent her home. Nobody comes to talk with you afterward. Nobody tells you your arm will swell up and that you won't be able to stand up straight. Nobody warns you it will hurt to drive. They just send you home, and no one knows what to say, so no one says

72

anything, and you're supposed to just go on as if nothing has happened."

She paused and stared at me.

"Yes, ma'am," I said.

"I went to buoy Corinne's spirits, tell her life goes on—which it does not—and do you know what she told me?" I shook my head. "Her husband is divorcing her, abandoning her for some little nitwit in his office. Do you know why?"

"No, ma'am."

"Because her husband can't stand to look at her now. He said that! He said, 'Your figure is ruined.'"

She started to cry, put her face in her hands. "It's the most appalling thing. Walking out on that poor woman before she's even healed. After thirty years of marriage. After bearing his children."

"Daddy would never leave us."

She stood up fast, switched off her tears, and leaned over in my face.

"Don't be so sure."

I drew my study board up close to my chest and turned away. You always felt sure she would slug you, or at least slap you hard, when she got that sudden squint-eyed look.

"Your father's been working a lot of nights and weekends."

I tried to imagine Daddy talking to a pretty lady at his office, sitting on her desk, touching her hand. The picture flickered like an old TV cartoon, then fuzzed out; instead, I saw him bent over his big desk sketching, reaching for his see-through ruler. That image was real, the edges on it were lined in black, clear.

"Are you going to help or not, Sarah?"

"What am *I* supposed to do?"

"Don't whine. I hate that whiney thing you've started. In answer to your question, there may be nothing anyone can do to prevent Edward from deserting us. And everyone in Atlanta will believe it's my fault because I'm a hideous freak now. Disfigured."

Daddy's *not* leaving, I thought, but didn't say it out loud.

"In fact, I think he's poised right now, ready to make a move, and the slightest thing could push him over, force him to go. That's why I'm asking you to please, please try to control yourself. I'm begging you, Sarah; you've got to straighten up."

"Straighten up?"

"If you don't behave, if you continue to carry on the way you have been . . . We must have peace in our house, Sarah. If we don't, I'm certain we'll drive him away." She pointed her finger at me and narrowed her eyes. "Mark my words."

And, as always, she closed the door as hard as she could. I wished the slam would cause a new crack that would keep dividing into other cracks, and that the ceiling would cave in and our whole house would fall in on itself. They would find us like they found the families in Pompeii, and the archeologists would talk about what each of us was doing when it happened. "The girl, approximately thirteen, appeared to have been reading some sort of textbook, perhaps in preparation for school. Of course, we can't be sure."

CHAPTER 7

On the night Mother said Daddy might leave us, I had a nightmare that woke me up screaming, "No, no," like you see in the movies. In the dream Ben and I are staying in a big, plush hotel. We have a suite with thick velvet draperies and gold rope tie-backs. There's a stranger in the room talking to Ben, an old man with a beard. Suddenly, all these people are barging in trying to take over our room. Ben pays no attention; he's in serious conversation with the bearded guy.

I look down and see that my skin has gotten very dry; it's cracking and I'm itching all over. I think if I can just get a shower and wash and wash I'll be OK. I step into the hall and begin searching for a bathroom, but every one I come to is full of laughing, unruly kids. They block the doors and won't let me in. Desperate, I run down some steps, but my feet are now deformed and I can barely walk. I'm hobbling on these melting-away feet and my skin is continuing to crack and peel off. I realize I'm dying. Good, I think, fine. Who cares. But then I think of Chris and Annie. They need me; I can't die.

I limp back to the suite. Our rooms have been stripped. My clothes, my old toys, books, everything is gone. Ben is there, not a bit upset. "They said we didn't check out in time," he comments. He's got a little duffle bag and he opens the door. The bearded man is waiting and they walk away.

I stand at the window and watch the truck pull off. I'm shivering, dying. I have no one, no possessions, nothing.

———•———

"Are you peroxiding your hair?"

"No, Mother."

"I see. So those yellow streaks are appearing mysteriously in the night."

"I used lemon juice last summer."

"Sarah, I won't tolerate this. You want to listen to sexually arousing music. You want to have dates and carry on like a college student. Now you're struggling to look like a floozy."

"I don't dye my hair."

"Why do you imagine I would tolerate your lying? I saw that shampoo you're using. It distinctly says, 'Adds blond highlights.'"

What could I say?

"I've thrown it out," she said. "You have beautiful hair and I won't let you ruin it."

Then she started on my clothes. Straight skirts were no good; my hips were getting too big. I should wear shirts under my sweaters. And my hair was wrong. Get it out of my eyes; pull it back off my face.

Even though Ben had been gone for months, I still ran toward his room after Mother's attacks. I'd head that way, then freeze like Simon-Says remembering he wasn't there. Once I went to Annie. She was on the floor between her beds coloring.

"Hey, Rembrandt, can I come in a minute?"

"Yep."

"Annie, how do you think I look in this color?"

She glanced up and scrolled her eyes over me.

"Fine."

"Mother says the color's totally wrong for me." I imitated

Mother's tone. "It's too bold. It overpowers your peaches-and-cream complexion.'" Annie didn't laugh like Ben would have. She shrugged and started coloring again.

"Sorry, I'll leave you alone."

Annie never mentioned anything going on in our house. I guess she had enough worries with Mother policing every morsel of food she put in her mouth. I'd trade with her though. That was nothing compared to having everything you said and did picked apart.

I thought it couldn't get worse till I borrowed Wendy's record "Come Softly to Me." Mother took it, said it was suggestive. I had to fork over my allowance to Wendy two weeks in a row to pay for it.

On the day she took that record Mother announced another rule: I couldn't close my door, ever, unless I was getting dressed or going to bed for the night.

"Why?" I asked.

"You can't be trusted."

I narrowed my eyes at her.

"This is a bed you've made. Now lie in it."

An odd thing happened. With my bedroom door always open, my ceiling seemed lower. It didn't make sense. And when I went into other rooms in the house, they felt smaller. The hall between my room and Annie's room got tinier too, more narrow. I slipped up to the attic, but didn't stay; it was hot and stuffy. I had no one to talk to. I never went to Wendy's anymore. She never had problems and I knew she was sick of hearing about mine. Sometimes, she'd sigh; mostly she changed the subject.

When I went to Daddy, he would look up from the newspaper, listen to the story, and tell me what he thought. Like when Mother said I should get rid of my coral sweater set, my favorite. "You look nice in that, Sarah. Very nice." But he never told Mother to get off my back.

I wrote to Ben too, waited and waited for advice. But his next letter came and there was nothing in it about my problems.

The night the solution came to me, I was lying in my bed listening to the holly bushes scratch on my window screens. I had my window open, a breeze was blowing my blinds in, and I got the idea.

I crept to my closet Indian-style (toe down, toe down), slipped on shorts, a shirt, and Keds. Then, oh so quietly, I arranged two throw pillows, my bed pillow, and my stuffed elephant under the covers. Strung out in a line, they were exactly the length of me. Getting out was a snap. Ease under the Venetian blinds, unlatch the screen, start out feet-first on my bottom; halfway out, flip over and slide to the ground. Ta-da! I fitted the screen back, but left a twig in it so it wouldn't shut all the way.

The next hurdle was getting my bicycle out of the garage and up the driveway, creeping along. At Mrs. Hendrix's, a few houses down, I took off. Pedaling fast on Valley View with the wind flapping my shirttail, I had no idea where to go. It could be anywhere, really, but I had to get back before the sun came up.

As I coasted down the big hill on Mabry Drive, I looked up at the charcoal dome of sky and thought about the terrariums we made in fifth grade. I hadn't wanted to put a lid on mine, but Mrs. McLaughlin said you needed it to make the plants grow. If the whole world is like a giant terrarium, I figured it should have a lid that's far, far overhead like tonight. I hadn't done "no hands" in ages, but that first night careening down Mabry with my hair shot back by the wind, I let go of both handlebars and reached straight up as high as I could for as long as I could without crashing.

Night after night I sneaked out and rode around our neighbor-hood, the back streets, the little cut-throughs you learn as a kid. Then, when no cars were in sight, I ventured across Peachtree to Garden Hills. Each trip had a destination: ride by Laurie Riley's house, or Chip Polk's, or the water tower on Lindbergh Drive.

"I passed your house last night," I told Phil in the cafeteria.

"Where were y'all going?"

"Not y'all. Me on my bike."

"Why didn't you knock?"

"Phil, it was midnight. The house was dark."

"Sarah!"

Phil wanted in when I told him what I'd been doing. He figured out how to slip out of his house that night, and we met by the Garden Hills pool, which was empty and the fence around it locked. But we sat on the swings at the playground, and eventually crawled into the tunnel part of the playscape so we wouldn't be seen if a car passed.

Phil met me every time I went out after that, two or three nights a week. We never went on weekends because my parents stayed up late, and there were too many people on the roads anyway. Eventu-ally, Phil asked if his friend Jimmy Edge could ride with us.

"Fine with me, but he'd better not tell anybody. Ever. If my mother finds out about this, she'll slam me in a cage forever."

The whole thing spread like kudzu. Jimmy Edge told Suzie Magbee; Suzie told her next-door neighbor, Pat; Pat invited David Blume. On any given night there were six or eight of us riding in a pack. Two of the boys wanted to get bold—stupid, in my opinion—and ride on Piedmont Avenue or Peachtree Road.

"No way. Y'all are nuts. I started this and these are the rules. No big roads. That's where the police patrol. If you want to get caught, go ahead, but you won't be with us."

David Blume argued but Phil backed me up.

It was the best spring. Mother kept criticizing me and ordering me around, but I didn't care because I'd be thinking ahead to that night, deciding whether to feed the ducks at Lakeview Circle or walk in Peachtree Battle Park.

Laurie Riley's sister Judy hung around with this strange senior girl named Vicki Ray. Every day at lunch, Vicki sat on the floor in the girl's bathroom in the gym surrounded by eighth-graders. She read their palms and told their fortunes with cards, and they waited on her like slaves, bringing her Krispy-Kreme doughnuts and Mars candy bars. She owned that bathroom; she and her worshipers eyed everyone who came in. They'd get dead quiet and stare at you till you left, and you knew they talked about you once you were out of earshot. I stopped going in there.

Laurie brought Judy along on one of our night rides, and Judy told us Vicki was holding a séance.

"What's a séance?" I asked.

"I'm not sure, but I think it's where you talk to dead people."

"Let's go!" Phil said. He loved *Twilight Zone* stuff.

Vicki and her brother, Alan, who was in my French class, lived in a big house on West Wesley. It was set back from the road with stone lions at the front of the driveway and a rolling lawn with enormous magnolias and Ponderosa pine trees. When we got there, Judy Riley tapped on the basement door twice and Alan let us in.

"*Bonjour,*" he said to me as we filed in.

I blushed and said, "*Non, bon soir.*"

Alan was handsome. He was tall and slicked his hair back like

Clark Gable, and he always wore starched shirts and gray slacks—no jeans.

We entered a downstairs den obviously set up for teenagers with a TV and a pool table. Candles flickered all around. Vicki wore a black robe and was sitting on a pile of pillows. She weighs about three hundred pounds and she'd put on a lot of dark purple eye makeup, cat-eye style.

A lot of kids called Vicki "Big Vick" behind her back, but I doubt she would care. She was president of the drama club and planned to study acting in Chicago after she graduated. She had set the stage for the séance well because it was eerie in there. I sat on the floor by Phil. Big Vick had us close our eyes and concentrate on bringing back a dead aunt of theirs named Edith.

"This is childish," David Blume said. "I'm going."

He got up and let himself out, shaking his head.

"Who else is chicken?" I asked, looking at each face in our semi-circle. Nobody moved.

"Pass this photograph," Vicki went on. "Study Edith's face. Hold the picture in your mind; then pass it along."

As we studied old Edith's face, Vicki chanted. It was a cloudy night, not much moonlight; our only light came from the candles. I noticed that the air in the room was still, yet the candle flames inched up and down, almost going out and then flaring up. Vicki told us to keep our eyes shut and continue to visualize Edith.

"Think about Edith's sweet face, her soft white curls. She's lonely on the other side. I sense her desire to join us here tonight. *E-ma-nee, nee patri mea. Tu-ma-nee, nee patri sui.* Mmm. Open your hearts to Edith. Cup your hands in your lap. Imagine them filled with love for Edith. For Edith and all the souls on the other side."

Vicki's husky, low voice and singsong words were relaxing.

I almost nodded off, but suddenly a little brass bell on the low coffee table in front of Vicki started jingling; I sat up straight. Vicki wasn't touching the thing, and I tell you it rose off the table and rang itself. Vicki's slanty eyes were clamped shut, but the rest of us were looking at each other bug-eyed. At that moment a flash of lightning outside lit up the room, and a chest-vibrating clap of thunder followed. Judy Riley shrieked and we scrambled to get out the door.

"Head for home, Sarah," Phil said from behind me.

I was already on my bicycle. Bikes clanked around me, and we wheeled away in every direction. I pumped harder than I ever had, bent forward like a jockey. I lived farther than anyone and was drenched when I slithered back in through my window. The bed was soaked; it was a miracle that the blinds blowing in and banging hadn't waked up my parents.

I stripped off everything, stuffed the ball of soaked clothes and socks in the back corner of my closet, and dug a granny gown out of my bottom drawer. In the middle of May, I lay there in a flannel gown shaking like a rattle.

all Annie and Chris to come in for dinner, Sarah, please. Your father will be here any minute."

Neither Chris nor Annie was anywhere in the house. I roamed the yard calling, and Chris finally appeared from the woods. "Time to come in and get ready for dinner, Chrissy-Chris."

"I gotta do somethin' with this," he said, proudly producing a teacup-size turtle.

"Neat."

He tore through the back door, slammed the screen, and darted back to his room.

"Where was he?" Mother asked.

"In the woods."

"Where's Annie?"

"I'm looking."

"Sarah, please. If you had any idea how difficult it is to time a meal . . ."

I checked the porch and the basement, but no Annie. The attic was the only place left. As soon as I opened the door I saw the light, so I went up and found Annie sitting on the cot eating a Moon Pie and reading *Peyton Place*.

"Give me that!"

She stared at me, blank, and handed it over.

"Come on, it's time for dinner."

She polished off the Moon Pie and followed me downstairs, still mute. "You're too young to be reading that," I said over my shoulder. Then I ducked into my room and wedged the book under my mattress.

"Where have you been, Annie?" Mother asked.

"Nosing around in my closet. Probably planning to filch something," I said. Annie looked at me, then at Mother.

"Don't start, Sarah."

Daddy came in halfway through dinner. By then the asparagus had gotten mushy and the roast was dry and crispy on the outside. Mother made a point of smacking and chewing hard like she was eating cardboard. Daddy apologized again for being late, but she chomped louder. Chris kept getting up, running back to his room, then back to the table. I knew he was sneaking food to the turtle.

"Are you ill, son?"

"Nope. I mean, no ma'am."

"Please stay at the table until we're all finished."

"How was your meeting today, Catherine?" Daddy asked.

"I didn't go. I may never go again. I can't stand listening to those hens cluck about their wonderful children. And I'm terrified someone will ask me about Ben. What do I say? 'Oh, Ben, uh, well, he won't call and he won't write, and for all we know he's driving a taxi.'"

Daddy opened his mouth to speak but she plowed on.

"Last month Kitty Lloyd yammered about Donald's wonderful grades at Rice, how he pledged Phi Delt. I was ill. Christopher, *please* stop playing with your food!"

"Darling, I've got to go to Wilmington for a few days," Daddy said.

"AGAIN?"

"We're competing with a Raleigh firm for the new high school. I'm sorry."

"You've never traveled so much. I think you enjoy it." She pitched her fork down and it clanged on the edge of her plate. "Chris runs wild day and night. Wouldn't it be lovely if he had a *father* around to ride herd on him? Sarah is completely out of hand!"

Annie hung her head, braced for what Mother would say about her. She folded her hands over her stomach, which would be the attack zone. But Mother stayed on Daddy.

"You're working later and later. You work all day on Saturdays; you're out of town constantly. I can't do this. I'm all alone! No friends! How could I have friends? I can't face people when Ben has done this to me."

Off to their bedroom, Daddy on her heels. Annie reached for a roll. Chris grabbed a handful of asparagus from his plate and vanished. I didn't want to leave Annie when she was upset; she'd keep on eating, and if she polished off the roast Mother would flip.

"Why'd Chris take that asparagus?" she asked.

"Oh, he found a turtle."

"I'm going back there."

The minute she got up the phone rang. It was Phil. "I saw Alan Ray at the drugstore; he's grounded. His parents woke up that night and found out everything. They took Vicki's car keys. She's grounded too—till she graduates."

"I better change phones, Phil. Hold on."

I raced to my room, took my phone off the hook, ran back to hang up the kitchen phone, and hurried back. I needed to know if Big Vick had ratted on us, but in split seconds Mother had materialized in my room. She stooped over between my beds unplugging the phone.

"Mother! I was on the phone!"

"You no longer have a phone."

"What did I do?"

She wheeled around. Mascara had run down her face and her eyes were swollen. Maybe I'll jump out my window now, start a bike ride early, I thought. I stood and faced her like a Buckingham Palace guard, my eyes unfocused.

"Do not touch a phone in this house," she said, and stomped away.

Phil was waiting for me by my home room the next morning. He looked worried.

"Are the Rays calling our parents?"

"No, Vicki didn't name names. Neither did Alan."

"Good. I'll see you in chorus."

Word had spread around school about our night-time rides and the incident at Vicki's. Kids I didn't know came up to me, asked if they could join us, when were we riding again.

"We're laying low right now," I said. I'd heard that saying on Hop-along Cassidy. No one seemed interested in taking any midnight rides anytime soon, especially Laurie Riley, who'd been caught and grounded too.

"I knew taking my sister would jinx it," Laurie said at lunch.

"It's not your fault," Phil told her. "Why don't we forget about this? Alan says Vicki is hacked off at us, but she's not going to report us."

"Thank you," I said, looking up to heaven. "It's bad enough having Vicki mad. If she can bring back the dead and cause thunderstorms, who knows what she might do for revenge."

"Wonder how Vicki rang that bell," Laurie said.

"It was her aunt's spirit," Phil said.

"Why don't I ask her?" I teased.

"You're nuts," Laurie said.

I was feeling confident because two more freshmen had walked up to our table to ask me about our next ride. After lunch I had English, and the restroom Vicki had taken over was on the way. She doesn't own that bathroom, I thought. I marched in ready to face Vicki and her circle of slaves, but there she sat alone, puffing on a cigarette. The little turncoats probably ditched her because she couldn't drive them around in her T-Bird convertible anymore. Once the wheels were gone, bye-bye Big Vick.

Vicki glared at me but I ignored her, walked to the mirror and started brushing my hair. I could feel her eyes on my back, but I kept brushing, then washed my hands slowly, slow enough to notice my fingers were trembling.

"Slimy sub-freshmen aren't allowed in here," she hissed.

I held my tongue.

"Go on, little kitty, scat."

With that, I ripped a paper towel out of the wall dispenser, wiped my hands, and spun around to look her in the face. "You know what you need to do, *Big Vick*?" I asked this in a tone I'd never heard coming out of my mouth. She looked surprised. Then I raised my voice and shook my index finger close to her nose. "You need to find another restroom. This one's *mine* now!"

She struggled to hoist herself off the floor, but I shot out of there.

Daddy's company got the job to design a new high school and gym in Wilmington, North Carolina. As the architect in charge of the project he would be away a lot, so it didn't look as if we'd have a summer vacation. Mother enrolled Chris in day camp and Annie in

Girl Scout camp before school even let out.

"She's getting antsy to get rid of us," I told Laurie Riley.

"Where's she shipping you?"

"I have no idea, but if she thinks it's Camp Blue Ridge again, she's wrong."

"No way I'm going back," Laurie said. "I'm working at Springer's stocking produce."

"How can you? You're only fourteen!"

"I know, but my dad knows Mr. Springer. I'm not looking forward to smelling like bananas all summer, but it's better than watching my mother get soused."

I went home with Laurie a few times after the Big Vick catastrophe; we played records in her room and practiced putting on makeup.

"I had some Persian Melon, but it dried out," I said. "Could I try some of this?" I picked up her lipstick.

"Sure, but it's not your color."

"Why not?"

"Too dark. You'll look like a hoodess."

People called guys who smoked and wore leather jackets "hoods," so Laurie and I referred to the cheap girls at school as "hoodesses."

"Hey, Laurie, what do you think really happened over at Vicki's that night?"

"The damn thing was rigged," she said, sweeping blue shadow across her eyelid.

"That's what I think."

Mrs. Riley tapped on the door, handed in some chips and French onion dip for us, and mumbled something.

"She's nice," I whispered after she left.

"She's bombed," Laurie said.

"Really?"

"Yep. Her coffee mug's got wine in it."

Something from Camp Blue Ridge came to Mother in the mail, but she didn't mention it.

She was being sweet, and it made me nervous. For no reason, she bought me a sketchbook, charcoals, and nice colored pencils in a wooden box you could prop up.

"You haven't put pencil to paper all year, Sally. Your talent is going to waste. I thought instead of hanging on the phone you might draw."

"I don't have a phone, remember?"

"Don't sass me, Sarah. I've just bought you a lovely gift."

I didn't know what she was up to, but I did sketch a giant Vicki, sitting Buddha-style in the center of the page. I encircled her with golden candle flames and colored her eyelids magenta. I loved my creation, but tore out the page and hid it in the back of the pad.

It didn't take long to find out I was being bribed. Mother had gone to her sewing circle—always intriguing since she didn't sew— and a crony said I could go to New Orleans with her family if I wanted to see Ben. I'm sure Mother figured I wouldn't want to go since I'd have to ride with strangers, so she had tricks lined up. The art stuff was one for sure. Another was leaving the brochure about Camp Blue Ridge on the kitchen counter.

"What's this? I'm *not* going back there."

"Sarah, please lower your voice."

"I'm turning fourteen this summer, and I'm *not* going."

"Well, Sarah, there is an alternative."

"What?"

"Penny Cabaniss—do you remember Mrs. Cabaniss?—Penny has elderly parents in New Orleans she visits every summer. Mr. and Mrs. Cabaniss would be delighted to have you go with them. You'd be company for their daughter, Alice, and you could see your brother!"

I wanted to jump up and cheer, but didn't. I had questions. Where would I stay? Would I stay with Ben?

"I don't know," I said.

"What do you mean, 'I don't know'?"

"How old is Alice?'

"Alice Cabaniss? Oh, ten or eleven."

"Gag. Would I stay with them or Ben?"

"You would stay in Mrs. Cabaniss's parents' home in the Garden District, Sarah, not in the French Quarter. But you would spend plenty of time with your brother."

I frowned. I wasn't sure I liked this plan.

"Sarah, you seem to search for some negative element in everything. Why don't you focus on life's positives, such as seeing your brother in this case?"

Who knows why I tried to discuss the trip plans with Mother. I knew I was going the second she brought it up. She carried on about what a "mahvelous" opportunity it would be for me to see a part of the South I'd never seen. But I'm not dumb. I knew she really wanted me to go down there, check out where Ben was living and who he was hanging around with. This was a spy mission, not an opportunity. Fine, I'd play her game, but I was going to make sure of one thing in the deal: no Camp Blue Ridge.

"Well, I guess I'll go. But I don't want to go to camp too."

"Who said anything about camp?" She laughed.

All the plans for the trip were made without me. It was Mother talking to Mrs. Cabaniss, and Daddy talking to Ben. Ben wrote to me and said he was glad I was coming down; he promised to show me all the sights. He also gave me a book-reading assignment. He'd just read *The Metamorphosis* by Franz Kafka and wanted me to get it and read it before I got down there.

The Cabanisses were leaving on a Wednesday and coming back on a Tuesday. Ben worked for an architect building models, so I would only get to see him in the evenings and on Saturday and Sunday. I pushed again to stay at Ben's apartment. If I could stand up to Big Vick, I could stand up to Mother. I lost.

Mother took me to meet Alice before the trip. She was eleven but seemed younger. She collected storybook dolls, and when she led me back to her room to see them, I pretended to be interested. It was so miserable growing up in the South where you have to grin and go "Oh, isn't that nice," when all the time you are bored cross-eyed and dying to say what you really think, like, "Grow up. No one cares about your Flamenco doll from Madrid!"

My friend Laurie said I didn't seem excited about the trip. "Aren't you glad you're going to see your brother?" We'd gone way out of her neighborhood on our bikes to the Dairy Queen and were waiting for our onion rings.

"Hell, yes."

I'd started cussing some, mainly around Laurie because she did.

"Well, what's the prob?"

"I met the daughter of the people I'm going with, and I don't think I'll survive with her along."

"What's wrong with her?"

"Nothing, that's just it. She's perfect. Her hair's perfect. Her clothes. If you said 'damn' in front of her she'd keel over. But the worst thing is she's eleven years old and still plays with dolls."

"Sounds like a lizard."

"What's that?"

"Somebody not cool. Look, just pretend you're asleep in the car and you won't have to talk to her."

"Thing is, I want to see the scenery. I read about the Mississippi Delta in *Baby Doll*, and I've been wanting to see it since I was twelve."

"What's there?"

"I'm not sure, but people run around in their underwear and grown women sleep in cribs on front porches."

"Good grief."

Mother made a huge to-do about my trip, as if *she* were going. She called everybody in her sewing circle, everybody in the women's altar guild at church, the whole garden club. She sent me on my bicycle to the A&P to buy mayonnaise, and the checkout lady asked me if I was packed yet. My Mother's mouth and her phone-dialing finger could reach more people than a billboard.

She chattered about what I would wear—in the car, sightseeing with Ben, to the nice restaurant the Cabanisses were taking me to.

"Is Ben coming with us?"

"I don't know."

"Mother, I want to be with Ben, not the Cabanisses every minute."

"Sarah, I feel sure Penny will invite your brother on every occasion, but I don't know that he'll accept. He has a mind of his own. Oh, Penny mentioned taking you and Alice to Lake Pontchartrain to swim."

I didn't want to think about swimming with Alice; I was worried that I hadn't finished Ben's "reading assignment."

"Mother? Have you read *The Metamorphosis*?"

"Years ago, and you have no business reading it. It's a disgusting story about a man turning into a cockroach."

"I know. But . . . I don't understand about that. What was—"

"You aren't taking that book with you. What would Penny Cabaniss think?"

The night before I left, I went with Phil Patrick to a young people's gathering at his church. They were serving dinner and showing the movie *Giant*. Afterwards there would be a discussion led by the youth minister. Mother didn't want me to go until she found out that Phil's uncle was driving us.

"Why don't you invite them to come a little early and I'll serve him coffee? Of course, he may want a cocktail. I could make a few hors d'oeuvres. I'm sure your father would like to meet Rod Serling. I want to ask him if he knows my old friend Helen Butler from college; she's been in television in New York for years."

The famous Rod Serling would not want to visit with my parents, I felt sure. Phil and I discussed it twice that afternoon, and he finally spoke to his uncle.

"Mother, Phil's uncle can't come in tonight. The Patricks are having company for dinner and Mr. Serling will have to get right back. He's driving us because Phil's parents will be busy getting ready for the dinner."

"Well, I have several things to ask him, Sarah, so you'll just have to be running a little late. I'll go out to the car to apologize."

That night she instructed me to "piddle with my hair" for ten minutes when Phil rang the doorbell.

"Ten minutes! Mother, we'll miss the beginning of the movie!"

"*Ten* minutes, Sarah."

When I finally came out, Chris was showing Phil his newest baseball cards.

"Your little brother's neat," he said as we walked out to the car. "What were you doing?"

I brushed him off. I needed to get to the car, where Mother was leaning over chatting with Rod Serling like she'd known him all her life. He was smiling and nodding.

"Your mother is a charming woman, Sarah," he said as we backed out of the driveway. I was speechless. "In fact, we know her cousin Isabel very well. She's a friend of my wife."

"Oh." I'd never heard of anyone named Isabel.

"What's your brother's book about?"

"Sir?"

"Your mother asked me to take a look at your brother's book when he finishes it. Is it a mystery?"

"Uh, I'm not really sure."

"Well, someone gave me a break when I was starting out. I'll see what I can do when he's ready."

Phil jabbed me in the ribs a time or two, but I spent most of the ride to the church with my mouth hanging open. I was appalled that my mother had lied about Ben writing a book. It was one thing for her to lie to her club friends, but Rod Serling!

Since Phil had already seen *Giant*, he wanted to skip it and just go in for the discussion at the end, so we cut through the kitchen and out the back door to a courtyard. "Wanna sit?" Phil motioned to a bench.

"Should we be doing this?"

"I don't know, but I won't be talking to you for a while. You're leaving and we're going to Connecticut to see my grandmother just before you get back."

"True. Hey, what was it you had to tell me?"

"Oh, I saw Alan and he finally confessed what happened at the séance that night. But we can't tell anybody. He said Vicki would kill him if he told."

"Told what?"

"The bell was rigged. Before we got there, Vicki had Alan run black thread through the top of the bell, and then up and over the light fixture. All she had to do was wrap her finger around the thread and wiggle it, and the bell would lift up and ring."

"That girl is sick," I said.

"Well, it could have been spirits," Phil said.

"I guess."

Phil liked to believe in magic. He loved to wonder how the pyramids got built, and Stonehenge. I didn't want to disagree with him, he seemed so disappointed about the hoax.

We sat there for awhile and Phil held my hand. His was much rougher than mine, but warm.

"Sarah, will you wear this?" He let go of my hand, reached in his pocket, and pulled out a heavy silver I.D. bracelet with Philip engraved on it in block letters.

"You mean, go steady?"

"Yeah."

Mother's face popped up in my brain like a jack-in-the-box, her nostrils flared.

"I better not."

His face fell.

"I'd like to take it. I love it, but Mother would murder me."

"Couldn't you wear it when you're away from home?"

"I'd have to hide it, and she goes through my stuff. I know she does. She'd find it, believe me."

He sighed and put the bracelet on his own arm. He acted weird for the rest of the night. I just prayed that when I got home she wouldn't grill me about the movie.

Fortunately, she was on the phone when I came in.

Oh, Amelia! I was supposed to call you. Please forgive me; we've been frantic getting Sally ready to go to New Orleans.

Yes, it will be an experience. Penny's parents live in the Garden District, and they're taking her to Commander's Palace. What was that? Oh, she can't wait to see Ben. No, my heavens, he lives in the French Quarter. He wants her to stay with him, but a bachelor pad is no place for a teenage girl.

Midge Grayson called from The Journal, *by the way. She wants to write it up in "Social Whirl."*

"What's that? Oh, I have no idea who told Midge, but Sarah's delighted! I'm sure she'll want the clipping for her scrapbook."

CHAPTER 9

The Mississippi Delta was a letdown. Mr. Cabaniss said there wasn't much to see there. Of course, we went through it in the dark, so I can't be certain that's true.

They wanted to leave in the afternoon and drive in the night to avoid traffic. A great plan, as it turned out, because Alice and I slept a lot and didn't have to talk. The world of an eleven-year-old girl is strange—still a kid but pretending to be a grownup. It's like a twilight zone. Realizing this made me understand why Annie and I had so little to say to each other. I'm not claiming I was a grownup either, but I wasn't interested in kid stuff anymore.

"Give Ben a big hug for me, Sally," Annie had said as I left. "But don't kiss him if he has one of these!" She stuck a picture of a bearded beatnik in my hand that she'd torn out of the newspaper, along with a letter for Ben.

"OK. If he grew a beard I'll just hug him and tell him you don't like him anymore."

"Sally!"

"Only kidding."

Ben having a beard never crossed my mind. I was thinking about how to convince him to come home, at least for a visit. Or call. It wasn't a picnic at our house before he left, but it was hell on earth now. All Mother did was scream at us or cry. Chris stayed outside or at friends' houses, so he probably didn't notice. But Annie seemed miserable, Daddy was gone most of the time, and I was a prisoner, a worm in a glass jar who slimed out every now and then at night.

After we loaded up, Mother went inside to get a pillow for me. Alice and I were in the back seat, and she had one. I opened the door to take the pillow, and Mother noticed my book for the trip. *Wise Blood* by Flannery O'Connor.

"Isn't that a little mature for you, dear?"

"Ben left it. I'm taking it to him."

She sighed. She didn't fool me; she didn't care what I was reading. Her concern was what Mrs. Cabaniss would think. What people *thought* about the Claibornes was more important to her than anything.

We stopped for dinner somewhere in Alabama, a place called the Dutch Mill that had a phony windmill next to it. Nobody should make the mistake of eating fried chicken on a long car trip. I did, and it turned into a bowling ball in my stomach. It was a metamorphosis, I guess. When it got too dark to read anymore, I stuffed my pillow against the door and used my sweater as a blanket. "Would someone wake me up when we get to Mississippi?"

"Any special place?" Mr. Cabaniss asked.

"The Delta."

"It's a big area," he said, business-like. "Miles and miles of flat farmland."

"So there won't be much to see?"

"Honey, when we drive through Mississippi it feels like we're in the middle of nowhere. The highway was built away from most of the towns. I make sure to have a full tank of gas before we cross the state line."

Tennessee Williams must have imagined what he wrote about the Delta being so unusual. Or maybe people really are wild there because they're bored. Or hot! My only memory of that state was stepping out to use the restroom at a combination gas station, food store, bait shop. Going from the Cabanisses' air-conditioned Oldsmobile into the Delta air felt like somebody had dropped a steaming blanket over the world. No wonder Baby Doll slept out on the porch.

When I opened my eyes and realized we were on the outskirts of a city, the bowling ball in my stomach was gone. Now it felt empty and fluttery.

"Is this New Orleans?" I asked, my voice froggy.

"Won't be long. We're about fifteen miles away."

When we got there, Mrs. Cabaniss suggested we drive through the French Quarter and locate Ben's apartment, although he would be at work. She fumbled around in her pocketbook and pulled out a piece of paper, then dug in the glove compartment for a map. Alice woke up and started combing her hair; I did the same.

"What's your favorite thing to do down here?" I asked her.

"Play in Gramma's backyard. She's got a neat pond with goldfish."

"Umm."

Mr. Cabaniss pulled up to a building that looked like the saloon in *Gunsmoke*, a big wooden thing—two stories—with no paint on it and a tin awning over the sidewalk in front. What was left of the sidewalk, that is. It was cracked and the dirt had risen up through it. There were no people around, just empty-looking buildings.

"Could this be right?" Mrs. Cabaniss asked her husband. Her voice was heavy.

"*This* is where my brother lives?" I asked, sitting up straight.

"These warehouses look abandoned," Mr. Cabaniss said and consulted the map again.

Just then a bus pulled in behind us. A fat lady with yellow hair in a pony tail on top of her head got off and walked toward the building. Mr. Cabaniss rolled down his window.

"Excuse me." He cleared his throat. "Ma'am?"

The lady turned around. She looked hopeful, like she'd been expecting somebody for a long time.

"Ma'am, I'm sorry to bother you. Is this 1809?"

"Who ya lookin' for?"

"Uh . . . Ben Claiborne."

Her face fell, but then she quickly put on a phony smile. "Ooo, yessir. Why, yes he does."

She walked over to our car. She had on red high heels. Really high. One of them caught in the broken sidewalk and she pitched forward. Then she leaned over to look in the car and you could see down her blouse. I looked away, over at Alice. She looked away, too, and stared at her dad.

"You must be Benny's, er, Ben's little sister, come from Atlanta." She was pointing a long red painted fingernail at me. Mr. Cabaniss started to say something but Mrs. Cabaniss took over.

"Thank you very much. We'll be bringing Sarah back tomorrow. We wanted to make sure this was the right place."

"Oh, this is it. You just go up those steps. I'm A, right here. He's B."

"Thanks much," Mr. Cabaniss said and began to pull into the street.

The lady stood there, sad-like, and watched us leave. How could Ben live in *that* place. Or be friends with *that* person. She looked like one of the people at the Southeastern Fair, the ones who collect tickets. "Frowsy," my mother would say.

Everyone was quiet. We sure couldn't sit there chatting about Ben's nice neighborhood. I knew the Cabanisses were shocked.

Another humiliation for Mother. Maybe they wouldn't mention it to her; maybe she'd never have to know.

We were out of the Quarter in a few minutes and heading down a wide boulevard called St. Charles Avenue. Streetcars clattered up and down the center. "Wonder if one of those is the 'Streetcar Named Desire,'" I said, to fill the silence.

"Honey, there's not a streetcar named 'Desire' anymore. It's a bus now," Mrs. Cabaniss said. "In fact, we saw it back there in front of your brother's apartment."

"Oh." Another disappointment.

"We'll ride on a streetcar here on St. Charles before we leave though. That's a promise."

She was being extra nice to me. "Why would you name a bus 'Desire'?" I asked.

"Desire's a neighborhood, dear. The bus takes you there."

I tried to fit that in with what I remembered about Tennessee Williams' play, but it didn't make sense. He had misled readers about the Delta too. It was sort of dishonest. Like Ben in his letters, pretending he lived in a cool pad. It was a slum. I felt like an idiot in front of the Cabanisses. I wanted to cry, which I wasn't going to do in front of Alice. Instead I sat there making small talk about the beautiful homes we were passing.

"This is the Garden District," Mr. Cabaniss said.

"Real nice," I said. "Wonder why Tennessee Williams never wrote about *this*."

Grandparents are a mystery to me. In the movies they have sparkly blue eyes and snow white hair, and adore their grandkids. I have only one grandparent, my grandmother Claiborne in Savannah; she doesn't fit this description. Her eyes are hazel, they don't twinkle, and she's mean. People in my family treat her like delicate crystal. They say she's "eccentric." Truth is, she's mean and grouchy; I think she hates children.

Waiting for us in a big gray stone house surrounded with yellow flowers were Alice's movie version grandparents. The Duprees were short and looked like Mr. and Mrs. Claus. They complimented me from the time I got out of the car. How pretty I was. How tall and willowy. My, what lovely skin. Mrs. Dupree would say it, and Mr. Dupree would bob his head in agreement. Then they'd both chuckle. Lucky Alice. She got to come see these people every Christmas and summer.

Ben didn't call us till he got home from work at six. By that time I was so tired I was dizzy, so I wasn't mad when he said he wouldn't see me till the next night. He would come to the Duprees' straight from work and we would all go out to dinner. Mr. Cabaniss gave him directions. He was to take his usual bus from work, but after he changed to the streetcar, he'd catch a different one to the Duprees' corner.

"We'll come pick you up," Mr. Cabaniss said, but Ben told him he was used to walking.

Good thing Ben didn't come that first night. I felt flat and lifeless as a paper doll. But after a long sleep in the Duprees' cozy bed and a day lolling in their backyard, I was like the Road Runner in the cartoon.

"Whatcha doin', Alice?"

"I've been trying to count the fish, but the water's so dark and they keep darting around."

She was on her knees, bent over the pond.

"What are y'all going to do all day tomorrow while I'm with Ben?"

"Momma and I are going shopping at Maison Blanche and then have lunch at Gallatoire's or Antoine's. You may have to go with us."

"No. I'll be exploring the French Quarter with Ben."

"If Momma lets you go."

"What do you mean, 'lets me go'? The whole reason I came here was to be with Ben!"

"I know, but I overheard Momma talking to Gramma this morning about how she was responsible for you and that your mother would never forgive her if anything happened."

I wanted to storm in, demand to know what was going on. Instead I took off down the street in the direction of St. Charles. As soon as I spotted Ben, I ran toward him. He gave me a hug and I burst into tears.

"Sarah, what's wrong?"

"We saw your apartment and the Cabanisses think it's in a bad section and might not let me come see you there tomorrow and the only reason I came down here—"

"Sarah, slow down."

The Cabanisses discovered what a nice, normal guy my brother was, and once he assured them I'd be fine they seemed OK about the whole thing.

"I'm going to show Sally all the usual touristy things," he told them. "We'll go for café au lait and beignets in the French Market. And we'll walk around, and do a little people-watching too."

Mrs. Cabaniss smiled. "You'd better wear comfortable shoes, Sarah."

Ben looked good. He had on a sports jacket and a tie, and he hadn't grown a beard. I caught Alice staring at him. Probably she was jealous because she doesn't have a brother.

"Are you taking Sarah on a Mississippi river boat ride?" she asked him.

"I don't think we'll have time on this trip," he said.

"Aw, please, please," I whimpered. But I didn't really care about a river boat trip. I just wanted to be alone with Ben so we could have a heart-to-heart talk.

CHAPTER 10

Mr. Cabaniss drove me to Ben's after breakfast on Saturday. The quarter was crawling with tourists and we had to park a block away. I told Mr. Cabaniss he could drop me off, but he wouldn't. The yellow-haired lady was sitting out on the stoop looking unhappy. "How ya likin' New Awlins?'

"Fine," I said.

Mr. Cabaniss nodded at her and we scaled the steps to Ben's. The door was open but the screen was locked, so I tapped. Ben appeared from another room and welcomed us in. He was up and dressed but his shirt was wrinkled. He ran his hands up and down over the front of it. "No iron," he said, and laughed. "Well, this is it. Want the fifty cent tour?"

He took us through the apartment, which didn't take long. It was two big rooms and a little bathroom. The first room had two chairs, a card table, and a lamp by the front window. At the back end was the kitchen. Ben had a metal table and chairs between the sink and the wall with the stove and refrigerator. A few dishes were drying in a yellow wire rack on the counter.

"Coffee?" he asked Mr. Cabaniss, raising the white mug in his hand.

"No, no, we've just finished a big breakfast."

Like the first room, the bedroom had high ceilings and big windows across the front. There was a single bed—unmade—and a bedside table Ben had rigged up by stacking books and plopping a

Coca-Cola tray on top. He had a tensor study lamp and a travel clock on the tray. For a chest of drawers, he had cardboard boxes lining a wall. You could see all his underwear and pajamas and shirts.

"Look at this old tub," I exclaimed, to get out of there. The bathroom wasn't too bad, except the linoleum was an icky green and curling up in the corners.

That was it. Ben's apartment was old and bare, but clean. I wouldn't have wanted to live there with no TV, no radio, no nothing. And something told me that ancient spiders were lurking behind things. Mother was right when she said he'd gone down to New Orleans to be a beatnik.

"That's what I do in my spare time," Ben said, pointing at a beat-up metal chair on the landing outside his door.

"What?" I asked.

"Sit and watch the barges and river boats pulling in and out. I've got a good view."

Whoopee, I thought. No way would I tell my mother about Ben's apartment. She'd lie down with a sick headache and never get up. She worried when toilet paper wasn't color-coordinated with the bathroom walls, and she believed in having fresh flowers on the dinner table. On Ben's beat-up old kitchen table there was only a stub of a white candle stuck on a saucer.

After Mr. Cabaniss left, Ben fixed me a Coke and we sat down at the kitchen table.

"Well, how do you like my home-sweet-home?" he asked.

"It's neat," I said, enthusiastically. I don't know why I lied when Ben had always been the one person in the world I could be honest with.

"It was uncanny how everything worked out when I got down here. I went right from the bus station to the YMCA and got a room.

I had a plan, mapped it out on the bus coming down. Get a room at the Y. Buy a newspaper. Find an apartment in the Quarter. Find a job."

"Why'd you pick New Orleans?"

"I thought I told you."

"Un-uh."

"A friend of mine from high school was down here at Tulane; he said all these great things about the place."

"So he showed you around and—"

"No. When I got down here he'd just gone back to Atlanta. He'd flunked out!"

"So you didn't know anyone here?"

"No, but then I ran into Dizzy Darla and she told me about this place."

"Who?"

"Dizzy Darla. She lives downstairs."

"That fat lady with the fuzzy hair?" I asked.

"You saw her? Yeah, she works on Bourbon Street at a strip club. But she can't strip anymore; she had an operation that left a long scar across her stomach."

"What'd you call her?"

"Dizzy Darla? Oh, my friend Russell started that. She's not too bright. Anyway, she ended up getting a job as a shill at the club where she used to dance."

"A shill?"

"Yeah, she stands outside annoying tourists, gives 'em glimpses of the women inside. Cracks the door, then says they'll have to pay to go in and see more."

"How'd you meet her?"

"Oh, well, she tried to lure me into the place. She said, 'Hey, buddy boy, we got what you need right here!' So I said, 'Really, you've got a room to rent?' 'Naw,' she said, 'but we got some pretty ladies.' I told her I wasn't interested but she followed me, said there was a vacant apartment in her building. So here I am."

He went on about how great his job was, how his boss had taught him so much. I was dying to tell him about my night bike rides, and the séance, and standing up to Big Vick. And I wanted to discuss *The Metamorphosis* and the Mississippi Delta, but it seemed like he was going to tell me every move he'd made in the past six months.

"Oh, look, I forgot," I interrupted, and jumped up to get my pocketbook. "I brought some pictures of Chris and Annie to show you. There's Annie with the kitty from down the street. And that's Chris playing Ramar of the Jungle with his friend Mike."

I had about six pictures. Ben flipped through them smiling and shaking his head, kind of like, "Oh, those kids," but he handed them back to me and went on with the story of his life.

I wanted to scream. Ben had totally forgotten about me and Chris and Annie. Everyone back in Atlanta. Even Connie. He hadn't asked a thing about her.

"Hey." A tall, thin guy with black hair about Ben's age poked his face against the screen door.

"Russell, what's going on?" Ben leaped up from the kitchen table to unhook the latch to let the guy in. He seemed happier to see him than he had me.

"Just stopped by to see what you were doing. This must be little sis from Atlanta." He stuck his hand out to me; it was covered with something dark blue, like ink. I shook it anyway. Ben dragged a chair from the front part of the room for Russell, and they started talking about the cover of a book by Camus—what did it mean, and so on. I was left out since I hadn't read it, but then Russell turned to me and said how much he'd heard about me, that Ben said I was a cool sister. I felt better.

Russell was an artist. He painted the one and only picture that Ben had hanging in his apartment. It was different, a white drawing of a half-man, half-monkey on a black background.

The creature had a long neck and skinny legs. Pliers and tin cans and roller skates floated around him. I wanted to know what it meant, but didn't want them to make fun of me.

"You're good," I said.

"Russell sells his work in Pirate's Alley."

"Yeah," Russell said, "and I need to be down there today, but . . ."

"Why don't you come with us?" Ben suggested. "Sarah's seeing the sights today."

When Russell said sure, I had mixed feelings. I wanted Ben to myself but Russell was nice and said we could stop by his studio. I thought Phil and Laurie would be impressed to hear I'd visited an artist's studio in New Orleans.

"We'll do a lot of walking today, Sarah, but it's the best way to see the Quarter," Ben said.

All day we strolled and peered in courtyards and watched the weirdos. One skinny guy with wild eyes was skipping along talking to an invisible person. About every three skips he'd turn around and look behind him, mumbling, ". . . mustn't let it . . . no, no, no . . ." as we passed. I looked at Ben. "Deranged," he said.

After we passed the Deranged Man we walked down a block of nightclubs and beer joints where Ben told me to walk fast and stick close between him and Russell. "Don't look at anyone," he said. "Look straight ahead." There were fancy ladies out in front of several of the places. They reminded me of Darla.

"More strip clubs?"

"Keep walking."

The ladies at one place were talking loud and struttin' around. One had long red hair and tons of makeup. She stopped in the middle of her conversation and looked at me. "Hey, sweet thing, why don't you come on over and introduce us to those good-lookin' fellas? Your boyfriends?"

"Or sugar daddies!" the other one, a big blond, said.

We kept walking fast, but for some reason I felt scared. I knew they were just flirting with Ben and Russell through me. But they seemed dangerous—especially the redhead. As we passed, the redhead reached out and plucked at Ben's shirt, right at his breast pocket. Ben shoved her hand back and kept walking, deadpan.

"What was her problem?" I asked as soon as we were far enough away that the women couldn't hear.

"His," Russell said.

"His what?'

"What was *his* problem?"

"Huh?"

"I might as well tell you," Ben said. "Those . . . er . . . women . . . are guys."

I looked back at them.

"Transvestites. Men who dress up like women."

"Why?" I was almost shouting.

"I have no idea."

That closed the conversation. We slowed our pace, and Russell and Ben chatted about all the patrol cars in the Quarter that day, while I relived the scene with the gross women. If they were men, why did they dress like hussies? Why didn't that one paw at me? Why did she—he—flirt with my brother? Why was she so angry? But the question that rolled over and over in my head was, "Should I tell Mother about this?" And the answer that kept floating up in the little eight-ball in my brain was, "Do not tell your mother. You can't!"

After we'd walked a few more blocks, Ben steered us into a little coffee house that advertised fortune tellers. "How 'bout we find out your future, Sal?" I loved that kind of stuff. Wendy and I got our palms read once. We sneaked over to the lady's house on our bikes and paid our whole month's allowance to have her tell us what we'd be when we grew up. Wendy was going to get married and have six kids, she found out, and I was going to be a concert pianist.

In the coffee house, two ladies sat in alcoves behind strings and strings of crystal beads—red, purple, and pink. Ben approached the one named Sue; she had on gypsy hoop earrings that touched her shoulders and wore orangey-brown makeup that made her look dirty. But she had pretty eyes. Blue. Almost purple-blue, and they were deep set in her face, so it was like she was looking out at you. Ben told her to give me the five dollar reading.

"Drink your tea, sugar, and then the leaves will tell me about you," she said in a hoarse voice.

I chugged down the tea and stared at the tiny mound of soggy goo at the bottom of the cup. How would she "see" something in that? She looked at the glob and then closed her eyes.

"A woman, brown hair. She's rocking in a chair. Dim light. An attic. She has baby things around her: a crib, a stuffed animal . . . a bear! A brown bear . . . old, worn out."

The hairs on my arms stood up. Last winter, just after Ben left, I went up to the attic to get my warm jacket from the cedar closet and found Mother rooting around in an old trunk of our baby things. She was surrounded by baby stuff—Annie's bassinet, Chris's crib, Ben's "teddy."

"She's rocking, she's cradling something in her arms."

"What is it?"

She rubbed her eyes. "She's holding the bear in her arms like a baby; she's singing."

"What do you see about *me*?"

The fortune teller said she had a strong image of me in a wedding gown, which didn't thrill me. She could say that to almost any teenage girl and be right. Someday they'd get married.

You don't get much for five dollars from a tea leaf reader. The only other thing she saw was a young girl and a boy with a baseball cap that fit the description of Annie and Chris.

"That's my sister and little brother!" I said. "What are they doing?"

"I see them on the front porch of a big house, like a plantation. They're sitting in big chairs. Dark green chairs."

"Hmm." I was frustrated. She hadn't predicted much. Ben came over and paid her when he saw me standing up. "Well, so are you gonna be a millionaire?"

"Naw, but there was a wedding gown and—"

"Ooo-eee. Sally's gettin' married," he chanted. Russell laughed.

"Quit it, Ben."

We fit a lot into the day. We stopped by a famous oyster bar where a friend of Ben's worked on the weekend, but they ran us off because we weren't eating. At Café du Monde we had beignets, which I could have eaten all day. Beignets are square doughnuts with mountains of powdered sugar on top. I saw the nightclub where Dizzy Darla worked, and when the doors swung open I understood why Darla couldn't work there anymore. The women were almost naked.

Mother would throttle Ben if she knew he had me on Bourbon Street. Once my father went to Las Vegas to an architects' meeting and told Mother when he came back about the go-go dancers being so young. He said it was pitiful how they had to do that to live. He said after the first night he didn't go out again with the other men. Daddy has a big heart and I think if he could've he would have adopted those young girls and brought them all back to Atlanta. Mother took what he said the wrong way and screamed about how she had to slave over a hot stove to feed his children while he was out gaping at nude women. Daddy hung his head, hurt. I'll never understand my father. How could someone smart enough to design whole buildings not figure out when to keep quiet?

All we did in the French Quarter was eat. We bought sandwiches the size of dinner plates called muffulettas for lunch, and ate them in Jackson Square. After that we went to Russell's studio, which he lived over, and he let me have a little painting to take back to Atlanta. Not a monkey-man picture like Ben's; the one I chose had bright-colored blocks and circles. A mosaic, he called it.

"It's beautiful. Thanks," I said.

"A beautiful painting for a beautiful girl," he teased and put his arm around my waist for a minute.

I never got to talk with Ben alone. Russell must not have had any other friends to hang around with because he didn't seem to want to leave us. The Cabanisses picked me up at eight, just about the time Russell was inviting us to his apartment for red beans and rice.

"I can't, thanks. I've gotta go, and I'm still stuffed from that moofa thing."

"Muffuletta," Ben corrected.

Alice wanted to walk along the river down by the French Market, but her mother said we needed to get home.

"I'm sure Sarah is walked out," she said.

"Yes, ma'am. We just ate and walked, and walked and ate all day," I said in a sing-song, make-everyone-happy-who's-listening voice. Mother's garden club and church circle ladies use it all the time. Laurie and I call it the Edna Empty-head voice. The tone itself says, "I don't have a care in the world. La-de-da."

Alice's grandma offered me homemade vegetable soup when she found out I hadn't eaten since afternoon. I turned her down. The day had exhausted me, and I wanted to take a bath and conk out. Which I did by nine-thirty. I was vaguely aware of Alice coming in and crawling in the other bed, but then I was gone. I woke up with a start in the midst of a nightmare. I was aware of making myself wake up to get out of the dream. In it I was dressed as a bride, marching alone down an aisle. Then the aisle became a sidewalk, and all along both sides were men with beards and cigars dressed up in wigs and tight outfits—flashy ones, red satin and royal blue taffeta. And they were laughing and poking at me. I was punching their arms, crying, and stumbling on the sidewalk.

Church bells woke me on Sunday, and I lurched up, thinking they were wedding bells. My feet throbbed and my head ached; I fell back with a groan at the same moment someone thumped on the door.

"Alice? Sarah? Girls, it's time to get up."

Alice's grandmother came in with a flowered metal tray with two glasses of orange juice and warm blueberry muffins. Her eyes were twinkly even in the morning.

"Morning, Gramma."

"This is service," I said, sitting up.

"Growing girls shouldn't go hungry."

Alice was going to early mass with her family and out to break-fast afterward. They would deliver me to Ben before church so I could spend my last full day in New Orleans with him. While Alice dawdled in the bathroom, I dressed and ran over in my mind what I would say to him. Maybe we could sit on his stoop and watch the boats and talk. My feet were too sore to walk much.

Mr. Cabaniss parked at the bottom of Ben's steps so he could watch me go in. Ben leaned out and waved and Mr. Cabaniss looked satis-fied, so I went in.

"Hang on a minute, Sal," Ben said and went into his bedroom.

"What are those lines on the back of your shirt?" I yelled to him.

"What?" He stepped out.

"Turn around. Those funny black lines across your back."

"Oh, I had to dry my shirt in the stove this morning."

"Ben! Those lines are from the oven rack? You broiled your shirt?" I giggled.

He ignored me and grabbed his wallet and keys off the kitchen table. "I'm treating you to breakfast at the best place in the Quarter, little sister," he said.

I didn't tell him I was full of muffins, which was just as well because by the time we'd walked to Freddy's Coffee Pot I was ready to eat again in spite of my aching feet.

"One fried egg sunny-side up," I said.

"That's all you want?"

"Yep."

Ben ordered eggs, grits, sausage, toast.

"I miss those banana pancakes you used to fix us."

His smile folded.

115

"Ben, Mother has been awful since you left."

"What am *I* supposed to do about it, Sarah?" he snapped.

"Uh, well, guess what *I'm* doing?" I confided in him about the night bike rides and the séance and everything, but instead of being impressed and congratulating me on sneaking out under Mother's nose all those nights, he lectured me, told me I was "foolhardy," something bad could happen to me. "The only bad thing would be if Mother caught me and I got locked up at night like I am all day!" I laughed.

"Sarah, I'm serious. You're being childish. Look at you; you look eighteen. Do you know what could happen if some crazy man picked you up?"

"Oh, Ben . . ."

"Do you?"

"I *know* about *that*. No way any guy's going to jump me. I'm like greased lightning on my bicycle! He'd pull up and I'd shoot out of there so fast he'd be scratching his head."

"You need to grow up, Sarah." Very sarcastic. He sounded like Mother! My eyes were full, but if I cried it would seem like I did need to grow up. Do not cry. Do not cry, I told myself. Then the food came.

"What would you like to do today?" he asked after the waitress left.

"I dunno."

"Russell's probably coming by."

"Oh."

If Russell was going to spend the day with us again, I couldn't wait any longer for the perfect moment to ask what I needed to know.

"Ben, when are you coming home for a visit?"

"I'm not, Sarah."

He might as well have flipped his hot grits in my face. "Why?"

"I don't want to go into it. I'm just not coming back. Ever."

"But Ben, you've got to." A lump of egg that was halfway down my throat got stuck. I swallowed hard. "I'm worried about Chris and Annie. I don't know what's going to happen to them. I'm scared when they're there alone with Mother; she's been acting so strange since you left."

"Mother's *always* acted strange. Nothing's changed."

"Yes, something has changed. She had cancer. Didn't Daddy tell you?"

"Yes."

"She came home . . . different. She cried and cried and stayed locked in her room. Now she's always screaming at me or crying."

"Sarah—"

"I think she's going to lock herself in her room sometime and never come out. And Daddy's going to have to get his toolbox and take the door off and—"

"I can't come home."

A tear started running down my cheek but I wasn't about to touch it. I hung my face over my plate and waited for it to drop off. "I don't see what 'the big deal' is about you coming home for a few days." My voice sounded far away.

"All right, Sarah, look. The night before I left, Mother was furious and drank a lot and said something . . . told me something."

"What?"

"Jesus! OK, I'll tell you. But then this case is closed."

I waited, holding my breath and staring at the little triangle I'd cut out of the egg, my sunny-faced egg that was turning orange and dry.

"She started ranting at me, said she was glad I was dropping out of college, glad Daddy didn't have to spend any more money on me because . . . I'm not their son. She said they adopted me."

"Oh, Ben, you didn't believe her!"

"Sarah, she showed me the papers."

"What?" My head throbbed. This had to be a joke.

"Ben, you look just like Daddy."

"Yeah, well . . ."

"I don't believe it. You aren't adopted. No way."

"Sarah, I'm not going back. I can't take money from them. And I don't understand why they never told me before. Mother said she would never have told me if I hadn't 'pulled out of Vanderbilt.' She said it was criminal for me to waste Dad's money like that when I wasn't even his real son. So whose son am I, Sarah? I have no idea and I don't know if Mother and Dad even know. Look, let's quit this now."

He sounded really angry and raised his voice. A fat lady with turquoise glasses at the table behind us turned around and stared.

"What does Daddy say?"

"I haven't talked to him about it. I just said I couldn't deal with Mother anymore. Do you know why I have no phone here? She called me, called me, called me. Bugged me every single day I was at Vanderbilt!"

So? I thought. Everyone's parents pester them, but they don't leave town and forget everybody they ever knew.

"It's a lie, Ben. I know you're my brother."

"Sarah, I'm sorry, but I did what I had to do; there's nothing else to say."

I went through the remainder of the day answering Ben and Russell when they addressed me and pretending to be interested when we went to Pirate's Alley. What I wanted to do was go back to the Duprees' and forget what Ben had said. Why should I worry? He didn't mean what he'd said. He would cool off and come home, maybe by Christmas. And the adoption business was stupid. I could go home and dig out his baby book and find his birth certificate and prove it to him. But my head hurt so bad two aspirin didn't help.

"Sally, why don't you go in my room and take a nap?" Ben said. "Russell and I can play chess."

"That's OK."

"Go ahead. We'll be quiet. You're tired out from the last few days. I think I overdid my tour guide job."

"I'm all right. I don't need to sleep. Maybe I'll go lie down and read though. Oh, I brought *Wise Blood* with me, but I left it at the Duprees'."

"Reading Flannery these days, huh?"

"Well, you told me to!"

"Listen, forget those tortured Southern writers. I'm reading the French now—Sartre, Camus. I'll make you a list."

He stuck a book called *The Stranger* in my hand.

"Sweet dreams," Russell said.

"I'm not going to sleep," I told him, forcing a smile. He winked at me as if to say, "Un-huh, sure."

I went off to read but fell dead asleep after skimming the description on the back of the book. When I came to, the room was dark. I could see a thin strip of light under the door but didn't hear voices. I felt like Gregor Samsa in *The Metamorphosis*—heavy, unable to get out of bed, my arms and legs numb. And Ben's apartment was exactly like I'd pictured the apartment in the book. I lay there imagining that someone would bring me a bowl of food, shove it in, and slam the door like in the story. I wouldn't be able to get up;

I'd lie in this bed until I dried out and died. Then they'd come in to get me and I would crumble into brittle pieces like a stepped-on potato chip.

The door opened and the light from the other room flooded in. I couldn't see who was standing there.

"Sarah?"

"Yeah?"

"Bet you're hungry."

I reached over and switched on Ben's tensor lamp. Russell walked in and closed the door behind him.

"How do you like *L'Etranger*?"

"Who?"

"*The Stranger.*"

"Oh, uh, I conked out."

Russell sat down on the foot of the bed—there was was nowhere else to sit—and said Ben had gone to the store. "I'm going to make jambalaya for us. You'll love it; it's Cajun. I hope Ben has a big pot. Course, we could go over to my place. It's a wreck . . . but who cares."

"How'd you meet Ben?"

"God, didn't he tell you the story?"

Russell told me he and his girlfriend had come down for a visit from Austin, Texas, and had gotten in a fight. He said she was driving and made him get out of the car. "Crazy girl put me out on 61. I thought she'd settle down, come back, but she didn't. I walked four or five miles before your brother came along."

"Ben picked you up?"

"Well, Ben and his boss. They were driving back from looking at a job site up in Baton Rouge. I was hitchhiking by then and they stopped."

"My mother says you shouldn't pick up a hitchhiker. He could be a murderer."

"Well, I'm not a murderer, am I?"

I laughed and Russell started to rub my foot through the sheet. "Bet these old dogs are tired, eh?"

I laughed again. I was uncomfortable and wanted to move my foot.

"Why don't you pull these feet out and let me really massage them?"

"Naw, they're all right."

"Come on, I've got a little sister about your age. How old are you, sixteen?"

"Fourteen. Next month."

"You've got a birthday next month? How about that." By now he'd untucked the sheet and was holding both my feet in his palms. I felt like a watch that was wound too tight. "Relax," he said.

"I can't, it tickles." I squirmed and drew my knees up to my chest, which popped my feet out of his grip. "I need to go to the bathroom."

"Well, go on, li'l sis, I'll wait."

I went in the bathroom and splashed water in my face and dried it on Ben's rough gray towel. My hair was sticking up in the back, so I looked for a comb. I didn't see one, so I did the best I could with my fingers. When I opened the door, Russell was right there. I jumped back.

"Scared ya?"

He stepped into the bathroom, put his hands on my shoulders, and gently turned me toward the mirror.

"Look at that."

"What?" I said, embarrassed to look at myself with his head over mine and him watching my face.

"*That* is a pretty girl there."

I stood looking at my own eyes, trying to decide what to say.

"In fact, that's a lovely woman, not a girl." He let go of my shoulders and dropped his hands to my chest. "A very beautiful woman."

He was whispering in my ear and I froze. I knew I should move, but strange electrical currents were shooting around in my chest and I couldn't breathe or think. He began moving his hands and kissing my neck under my hair. I spun around. "I better go put—"

"Relax." His hands went to my hips and he held me in place. "Relax, Sarah, I only want to kiss you good-bye. You're leaving tomorrow, right?"

He kept me backed up against the basin, and leaned down with his head tilted. Before I could budge he had his mouth pressed on mine and one hand cupped behind my head so I couldn't draw back. Then he poked his tongue deep into my mouth and I tasted coffee. I jerked my head back but his hand tightened and our teeth hit together. That's when he let go.

"I gotta get my shoes on," I said, charging out into the bedroom. "The Cabanisses are coming to pick me up. I've gotta get ready."

"You've gotta eat first, honey." He was right behind me. I grabbed my Keds off the floor, circled around him and out into the front room. "Calm down, honey, I just wanted a little kiss."

Ben walked in with two grocery bags and looked at me funny. I don't know what my face looked like. "You finally woke up," he said. "Well, Russell, get goin', man. You're the chef."

Part Three

A door slamming makes one jump,
but it doesn't make one afraid.
What one fears is the serpent
that crawls underneath it.

Collete, *Cheri*

CHAPTER 11

*Y*ou're awake," Alice said.

"Hmmm . . ."

"You've been asleep for hours. You won't be able to sleep later."

"Oh, yes I will."

"Think you overdid it, Sarah?" Mrs. Cabaniss asked from the front seat.

"No, ma'am."

"What did you and Ben do yesterday, sweetie?"

"Walked. More walking."

"No wonder you're bushed."

I spent the next hour or so sketching. I copied scenes from the postcards I'd bought for Annie, drew the gypsy fortune teller as I remembered her, a rough outline of Ben's apartment building—only I made it look nice instead of a slum. I added lacy New Orleans grill-work where there wasn't any.

We stopped for dinner in a two-traffic-light town in Alabama. Besides us, the only people in the restaurant were a couple with a baby. The husband looked just like Russell, and my stomach sort of flip-flopped. I ordered a cheeseburger and French fries, but ate only half the burger and a sweet pickle. In the ladies' room Mrs. Cabaniss put her hand on my forehead. "I hope you're not coming down with something. Catherine won't be pleased if I deliver you home with a bug."

"I'm fine. Just tired."

Back on the road it was too dark to draw, so I hunched down in my corner and closed my eyes. Alice seemed wide awake, but I didn't want to chat with her. After a few minutes, she giggled.

I looked at her. "What is it?"

"I hope you don't sleep with your mouth open again. A fly could fly in."

"Very funny."

"What are you girls talking about?" Mr. Cabaniss asked.

Neither of us said anything. I was embarrassed. I hate having to sleep in front of someone I hardly know.

Our house was dark when we pulled in. "Let's go on," Mrs. Cabaniss said. "I'll bring you back in the morning, Sarah. I hate to wake everyone."

"No, it's okay. I've got a key."

"Are you sure?"

"Yes, ma'am. I'd like to sleep in my own bed tonight."

"I know, dear, I understand."

Like a proper Southern belle, I thanked her for everything and said goodnight. I looked over at Alice, but could see in the street light she was sound asleep. Mouth closed. Mr. Cabaniss helped me in with my suitcase, and just as I shut the door and turned to tiptoe to my room, the hall door opened.

"Sally!"

"Hey, Daddy."

"How was your trip?"

"Fine."

He switched on a lamp. "Want something to eat? A glass of milk?"

"No, I just want to go to bed."

He pecked me on the cheek and patted my arm. "Night, honey,

glad you're home. We've got some good news for you."

"What?"

"You go ahead. You'll hear about it in the morning."

Why did he have to say that? I lay there on my starched pink sheets, which I'm sure Etha Mae put on *that* day. What could the good news be? Maybe Ben had thought about what I told him. Maybe he'd called to say he was coming for a visit . . . or moving home.

Mother wasn't in the house; I felt it the second I woke up. Etha Mae was singing in the kitchen, loud enough for me to hear from my room at the back of the house. "Shine on me, shine o-o-o-n me. Mmm, mmm, oh Je-uh-sus, you fill me."

"Hi, Mae."

"Miss Sarah! You finally wake? Lawd have mercy, chil', you slep' through breakfast and here it is almos' lunch time."

"Where's Mother?"

"Chil', she been off with Miz Riddle since early this mornin'."

"Who?"

"A real 'state lady. Miz Riddle."

"Where's Chris and Annie?"

"They at camp. Now sit down here and eat something, and tell me, how's your big brother?"

"Some homecoming I get, huh?"

"Ma'am?"

"Ben's okay, I guess."

"He gonna be surprised when he hear you all's moving!"

"Moving! What do you mean, Etha Mae?"

"Miz Claiborne's out right now with Miz Riddle lookin' for you all a new house."

"A new house! Why?"

"Lawd, chil', she got it in her mind you all gonna change schools. Don't you know 'bout all the trouble, Miss Sarah? People says it's comin' here, too, jes like in Mississippi."

"I've lived here all my life, Mother. All my friends are here."

"Sarah, please. We aren't moving to Texas; we're moving to northwest Atlanta—if I can find a suitable house."

"But why? Why do I have to go to private school? I don't want to leave North Atlanta. All my friends are there."

"You're taking the test at Howell on Monday, all three of you. We don't know if you'll be accepted. Well, let me correct that. I'm certain you and Annie will test well, but Chris . . . I don't know."

"I don't know one single person at the Howell School!"

"Lower your voice, Sarah. You may know dozens, dear. Everyone in Buckhead is pulling their children out of public school."

"Mother, I don't mind going to school with colored kids. Is that why you're doing this?"

"Ssshh! Sarah, please." She pointed to the floor to remind me that Etha Mae was downstairs. "That's not the point, Sarah. The point is, the public schools may be shut down. Closed. Orville Faubus did it in Arkansas, and there's nothing to stop Governor Vandiver from doing the same thing here."

While Mother traipsed through houses with Mrs. Riddle, I combed through ours looking for Ben's baby book. Annie's and mine were tucked in a trunk in the attic, but Ben's wasn't there. Opening mine was hard. What if there was nothing about my birth? What if I found out I was adopted? But there it was on the second page, a little pink card with Crawford W. Long Memorial Hospital at the top, my tiny footprint, and the time I was born at the bottom. Signed by Catherine Atwater Claiborne and Edward Ellis Claiborne.

I rummaged through boxes in the cedar closets, but no book for Ben. I needed to find it, tear out his card, mail it to him. Then he'd get over all this and move home, maybe work for Daddy. I was taking my baby book to my room when Mother suddenly appeared. "Where are you taking that, Sarah?"

"Laurie wanted to see it. I found Annie's too. She was so cute."

"When her eyelashes finally appeared." She smiled. "They were turned under at first; she looked like a mouse."

"Where's Chris's book?"

"I never got around to making it. Everything's in a shoe box somewhere, though. Even a lock of hair."

"Where's Ben's?"

"I have no idea," she snapped.

It was as if I'd never been to see Ben. Mother asked a few questions when I first got home, and she flipped through my drawings. But it wasn't the third degree I'd expected. Just as well; at least I didn't have to lie.

"What's this, dear?" she chirped one day when she saw the sketch of Ben's apartment with my addition of grillwork.

"Ben's."

"Hmm, just as I'd imagined it."

And then off she went with not one but two real estate agents. Mrs. Riddle wasn't finding houses Mother liked, so she'd visited her office. Suddenly, there was an extra person out looking for her. I imagine everybody in that office was terrified by her rattlesnake glares. How many people have *two* agents working for them?

"Ed, I think we've found it. This new person actually *listened*—imagine! She took me to three properties today, two of which would do. But the perfect one's on Westchester Circle."

The new house was bought before anyone but Daddy saw it, before our test scores ever came. Change blew in on us like a Kansas tornado. I know how Dorothy felt when her little gray home twirled away and she woke up in Oz. That was my birthday present: finding out we were leaving the house I'd lived in all my life. Oh, there was a chocolate cake, although my favorite is caramel and Mother knows it, but no gift to open, just a certificate to buy new clothes at Rich's. For entertainment I got to hear Mother rattle on about the crepe myrtles and azaleas in the new yard, how badly they needed pruning. Happy birthday to me.

"What if we don't get into Howell?" Annie asked Mother during my festive birthday meal. "Can we stay here in this house?"

"Let's not think that way, Annie. We're moving to a lovely new home, and you'll attend an excellent school. What a privilege!"

Phil Patrick wanted to take me to a movie that night, but I made excuses. I knew he'd be upset about us moving, and I wanted to put off telling him. But that wasn't the only reason I didn't want to see him. Soon after I got home from New Orleans, he'd called. The minute I heard his voice I thought about Russell and felt sick. I don't know why. Anyway, Phil seemed like part of some long-ago life.

Our new house was big, two stories, up on a hill. Daddy said it was Georgian-style. We couldn't move in until a lot of work was done on it. The house was fifty years old and the elderly couple who'd lived in it had "let it go," according to my mother. She was charged up about redoing the house, in a tailspin, on the phone every minute, darting out to wallpaper stores, combing through furniture catalogs.

When we all went to see it, Annie seemed even less enthusiastic than me. She walked through without smiling or saying a word. In her room she just looked up and all around.

"I know you don't like this rose-colored carpet, dear, so I want you to come with me to pick out something you absolutely love," Mother said to her.

"It's fine. The rose color's fine."

Probably best she left it to Mother. Annie was into brown at the time. She wore brown every chance she got, which is not good when you have brown hair and brown eyes. I chose bright yellow for my walls, and a cream and white striped wallpaper for my bathroom with little clumps of blue flowers here and there. "I love the paper, Sarah, but isn't that yellow a bit electric?"

What she meant was, "Choose something else. I hate that yellow." But I wouldn't budge. "You said we could pick our colors, and that's the one I like."

Chris ran up and down the halls, up to the attic, and downstairs to the playroom.

"This is not a ball field, Chris, slow down!" Mother called out.

The house had high ceilings, wood floors, and fancy tile in the bathrooms—the only things she didn't change. But every surface was repainted and re-wallpapered; the bedrooms and study got wall-to-wall carpet—"the newest thing," she said. The other floors were stripped and sanded and re-stained; old draperies were ripped down and replaced with shutters—"very Savannah"—the fireplace enlarged, the backyard terraced.

"Aren't you excited?" Laurie asked.

"Why should I be? If you can't have friends over, you might as well live in a cave."

"With all that room, maybe she'll let you have company."

"I doubt it. But she is letting us decorate our rooms the way we want."

"Are you going to Howell?"

"I don't know. We still haven't heard."

"How far away is the new house? Can we still meet at night?"

"It's a twenty-minute drive. Too far for bikes."

"Oh, well, I don't need to get in trouble again anyway. I just got un-grounded."

I wanted to talk to Laurie about Russell, tell her what happened. Every time I saw her I thought about it, but then I'd push it out of my mind. Off and on, throughout the day, every day, the scene would come back to me and I would feel nervous, so I'd think of something else, get busy. Then out of nowhere it would bob up to the surface like a cork on a fishing line.

I put everything away that reminded me of New Orleans—the postcards, my sketches, Russell's painting—crammed it all under sweaters on my closet shelf. What I couldn't do was stop looking at myself in the bathroom mirror. Each time I did, Russell's face would appear over mine and I'd relive the whole thing. A wave of fear would wash over me, but that prickly electric feeling would come back, the same one I used to get when I read *Peyton Place*. I knew I shouldn't look in the mirror. But there I'd be, brushing my teeth, purposely not looking at myself, when some force made me glance up and I'd go through the whole thing again.

he moving truck was arriving at nine o'clock. Mother woke us at 6:30 so we could eat breakfast, dress, and pack our last few things.

"Please strip the sheets off your bed, Sarah, and see that Annie and Chris do the same. Would you, sweetie pie?"

"Chris won't do that."

No response.

Okay, all right, anything to keep her from blubbering like she had at breakfast. She'd flounced around like Loretta Young for weeks, thrilled over the new house, and now she was weepy about us kids being born here. Not *in* the house, but while we were living here. I don't remember anything about Chris being born for some reason, but I remember Annie coming home. I insisted on sitting out on my red wagon in my snowsuit to wait for her. It seemed like hours, but they finally pulled in, and I rushed over to see the new baby. Etha Mae lifted me up to peer in and I squealed "ooohhh" so loud Mother shushed me through the car window.

I pulled off my sheets, then went to Annie's room but she wasn't there; Mother was. She was squatting in the corner, rubbing some dark brown stripes on the floor, sniffling. "These marks are from that rocking horse. Remember that horse?"

She always tried to drag us into her pity boat, but no one would ever climb in. Then she would carry on about how no one in the family had feelings but her. I wanted to throw her own lines at her that day, ask why she *insisted* on being so negative when this was such a "mahvelous" opportunity. Why, moving to Westchester Circle was a privilege.

"I'm glad we're moving. I've got a much bigger room and my own bathroom."

"You're absolutely right; off we go to a wonderful new neighborhood and we won't look back. But I will miss my Paul's Scarlets. Walk with me to see them one last time, would you, honey?"

I didn't want to, but I granted her that small request. Only we did more than kiss her roses good-bye; we toured the whole yard, front and back. She was proud of our yard. "Your father and I make a pretty good landscaping team, don't you think?"

"Yeah. Yes, ma'am."

"Look, look, honey, this was all bare when we bought this house. Just dirt and weeds." She swept her hand in a circle and slowly turned, admiring our front yard: the neatly trimmed English ivy lining the walkway, the camellia bushes, the dogwoods, and the roses. Roses climbed and crawled along the white fence that enclosed our yard. They were pretty, I have to admit, like something on the cover of one of her gardening magazines. Deep purplish red, weaving and winding in and out of the fence boards. No one else on our street had roses or sculpted hedges or flower beds galore.

We ambled down the driveway to continue Mother's guided tour of the Claiborne grounds. There was the rest of the family, Annie helping Daddy pack tools in the garage, and Chris circling the turnaround on his bicycle.

"One last good-bye to the yard," Mother sang out, as if she hadn't been boo-hooing minutes before.

Daddy said something to Annie and then walked out to join us.

"We never got around to that, did we?" She gestured at the area under the crabapple tree where there was no grass and only a few scrubby shrubs.

Daddy smiled. "No, but if you'll step right this way . . ." He put one arm around Mother and the other around me and ushered us under the arched trellis to the middle part of the yard, which was Mother's territory. Kids had to continue through it to the far back-yard where the playhouse was, and the sandbox and swings. In Mother's part, there were neat flower beds in rows around the outside of a square. In the center of the square was a circular garden lined with unusual stones and planted with roses in different sizes and colors. I suppose it was nice. I could see that now at fourteen. And I do remember Mother and Daddy smiling and laughing when they were working on it together.

"We had lovely parties in this garden, didn't we?" Mother said.

Daddy agreed and then set about trying to lift the stone sundial in the rose garden.

"Let the moving men do that, Edward, you'll get a hernia. What are you grinning at, Sarah? A hernia's not funny."

I was remembering the party Ben and I had ruined. We hid up in the chinaberry tree to spy, and then hissed at the bats; they had gotten excited about being waked up in the middle of the day and swooped down into the guests' hair.

We got to the new house first—Daddy, Chris, and me. I had about five minutes to stow my book satchel in the back of my closet. It had Russell's painting in it, all my letters from Ben, and the battered copy of *Peyton Place*—things Mother didn't need to stumble upon. A horn tooting told us Mother had arrived in her car. Annie was wedged in with two lamps, a silver chest the movers might try to heist, and Mother's autumn haze mink stole. They were barely in the door when the moving truck barreled up the driveway, bringing low-hanging pine tree limbs crashing down and setting off a neighborhood dog. Daddy determined the best entrance for each piece of furniture, based on its size and what part of the house it was going to. Mother wrung her hands and barked at the movers right along with the howling dog. "Please, *please* be careful with that curio, it's a hundred years old. Oh, my . . . watch it!"

When they nicked the Sheraton hunt board passing through the back hall, she threatened to call their boss. She also began scrawling notes on a pad. The men looked harried. Hot and harried. Had Etha Mae been there, she would've made lemonade for them. But she wasn't there.

"I don't understand this, Edward. Mae was to be here before we were. I gave her a key yesterday and explicit directions over the phone last night. She was to transfer at Five Points to the Oglethorpe bus, get off at Peachtree Battle, and change to the maids' bus."

The moment the first phone was plugged in, it rang. Etha Mae was stranded in downtown Atlanta. She'd missed two buses and was panicky. Daddy and I set out to find her. We'd left Mother in a snit, but we knew it wasn't Mae's fault when we got a few blocks from Five Points. There was a roadblock across Marietta Street, and backed-up cars.

"What in the world?" Daddy said.

Sirens wailed and up ahead we could see police officers, some on foot, some on horses. A policeman was coming down the line of cars speaking to each driver. When he got to us, Daddy asked if there'd been a fire.

"No, sir, we've got a situation here. You need to leave the area."

People in front of us were backing and scraping to do U-turns. Daddy put the car in park and jumped out to catch up with the officer. He spoke to him for a few minutes and then came back.

"What's going on, Daddy?"

"Some kids caused trouble at Rich's. The Klan's here."

"The Ku Klux Klan?"

"Sarah, I've got to find Mae. She's waiting for us next to Rich's."

He turned in at the Atlanta Journal-Constitution building and parked. "Wait here, honey."

"I'm not staying here alone!"

"Well, then stick close to me."

The sidewalks were filling with curious people who'd heard the commotion from their offices. Policemen were telling them to go back inside. Daddy had to talk to three officers before we made it to Rich's. The last one, a young guy, led us through the mess.

"Some Negro students were gathering," he told Daddy. "They were planning a 'sit-in' at the tearoom."

When we rounded the corner and started down the hill for Rich's, we could see the line of men in their white sheets and pointy hats, six of them holding hands so they formed a chain across the main entrance. A lot of colored people had bunched around them and were standing there not saying anything, just watching. In between them and the Klan men was another line of policemen. They were facing the colored people, hands on their billy clubs. It was so quiet it was eerie.

All of a sudden some people on the edge of the crowd started talking and waving their fists in the air. A big man in a red velvet robe had come around from the back of the store. He had on a tall black dunce hat with gold trim on it. Even though he had a thick beard, you could see he was scowling. He passed close to us and I got a good look at him. He had the meanest eyes I'd ever seen—solid black and beady, cold and hard-looking.

"Who is *he*?"

"The Grand Dragon. The Klan leader."

The man looked stupid to me, like a sunburned farmer dressed up in a king's robe and a wizard hat. His evil eyes made Mother's rattlesnake face seem like Bambi's.

The young policeman was able to thread us through the people to where Etha Mae had said she'd be waiting. And there she was at the bus stop, looking terrified.

"Lawd, have mercy, Mister Claiborne."

I hugged her, then Daddy took her arm and told her to come with us. The policeman got us a block away, then got called on his walkie-talkie and had to go. I clutched Daddy's arm and he guided Mae and me out of the area and about three blocks in the wrong direction to circle around the mob. Mae was huffing by the time we got to Daddy's car.

"I'm lockin' your door, Miss Sarah," she said from the back seat, and she leaned up to punch the lock on my side. Daddy locked his, not saying anything.

Mae was a wreck. Usually she was the calm one, rock-solid, always smoothing things out in the Claiborne household. She began to cry and Daddy pulled into a Jacob's Drug Store parking lot. He stopped the car and turned around. "Are you all right, Mae?"

"Yessir, Mister Claiborne, but my head be throbbin."

"I'll be right back, ladies."

In a few minutes he was back with a brown bag and a cardboard container with three Coca-Colas in cups. We sat in the car and sipped our Cokes, and Etha Mae took two of the aspirin Daddy had bought.

"Mister Claiborne?"

"Yes?"

"How am I gon' get home tonight?"

"We're going to take you, Mae."

It was a good thing Mother hadn't gone to pick up Etha Mae. Mother's idea of going to downtown Atlanta was to pull into the parking deck at Davison's, enter through the covered bridge, and proceed to the tearoom for a fashion show and chicken à la king served in swan-shaped pastry shells. A memory of my spoiling one of her outings when I was five or six is locked in my brain. We were to have a "girls' day out," just the two of us. She dressed me like a doll in a buttery-yellow dress, matching hat and coat, white socks, and shiny Mary Jane shoes. It may have been a special mother-daughter event at the tearoom; I don't know. But as clearly as if it happened yesterday, I remember telling her on the escalator that I needed to go to the bathroom.

"Why didn't you go when I asked you at home? Why do you do this to me *every* time?

We'll have to go all the way back down to the mezzanine." She stopped for a minute. "Oh, well, we'll just go on to the tearoom. Surely there's a ladies' room there."

She jerked me along, almost popping my arm out of the socket. By the time I'd gone to the bathroom and she'd combed my hair, flounced out my skirt, and re-tied my sash, the fashion show had started. The waiter seated us, and Mother glared at me. When he left, she leaned over and whispered in my ear, "You ruin everything, Sarah."

Had Mother driven downtown that day it would have undone her. As it was, she viewed the incident as a major inconvenience. "I can't believe those people would stage a demonstration on *the* day, the *one* day that we're moving."

The story about the incident ran on the front page of the paper the next day, but Mother didn't look at it. Establishing order in our chaos was much more important to her, and she continued to take the timing of the event personally. Back then, I didn't read newspapers, but when I saw the bearded man's picture, I did read the article. They referred to the Grand Dragon, but didn't say why he showed up that day. It turned out there wasn't actually a sit-in. Someone called the department store and said there was going to be one, but there wasn't. So the Ku Klux Klan members and police were there for nothing. Five people were arrested, but no one was hurt. In the story, a man from the NAACP predicted there *would* be sit-ins in Atlanta— all over the South—before long.

Yes, Amelia, we're finally settled. What an ordeal!

Oh, the children are thrilled to pieces. There's so much more space, you know.

Well, yes, he would have liked to build. He designed a house for us long ago, but all this school business came on so quickly, we had to act.

No, he's delighted. This is a lovely house, fabulous architectural detail. You'll have to see for yourself, Amelia. I want you to come by anytime. Please!

Now, enough about us. What about Frances and Matt? What if the schools do close?

Oh, no! You can't leave Atlanta!

Well, yes, we are blessed. They were all accepted, all three of them. They're tickled pink. It's an adventure!

CHAPTER 13

*B*ecause I'd been swept into Mother's moving frenzy, I'd forgotten about finding Ben's birth certificate. Now I wasn't sure I even cared. My world was flying apart, and he wasn't here to help. Besides, Mother was happier than I'd ever seen her. Maybe she'd finally gotten over Ben's leaving; maybe I needed to do the same. Face it, I told myself, he's gone and he's not coming back. Also, in some warped way I thought that Mother might start idolizing me now like she had Ben. I would become the crown princess in the absence of the prince.

In the meantime I had to figure out how to survive the Howell School, which was like attending a funeral on a daily basis. Drab uniforms, hushed halls—nothing like the din at North Atlanta, with kids laughing and banging lockers. Everybody had mandatory chapel Monday through Friday, even students who weren't Episcopalian. The teachers were unfriendly and formal, and they heaped on homework from day one. No "easing" into the school year. The campus was a half-mile from the Chattahoochee River, and by the end of first period that first day, I considered crashing out of the front doors and running to the river; maybe I could drift downstream to some other city, start over.

No one spoke to me all morning and I ate lunch alone, thinking about my friends at North Atlanta, imagining what they were doing at that moment. Phil would be in the cafeteria with Jimmy Edge, maybe Laurie. By now, he would know I was gone, moved away, enrolled in a new school. He'd be hurt that I never called him back.

I dreaded fourth period. Latin. Mother insisted I take it. She said Ben had an extraordinary vocabulary because he had three years of Latin. I'd heard him practicing: *hic, haec, hoc, huius, huius, huius,* over and over. Why learn a dead language? It seemed pointless.

I had plopped down in the back row in the corner, slid as low in the desk as I could without disappearing, when in walked Ann Odom, a girl I'd known in Sunday school since kindergarten. I hauled myself up, grinned, and waved at her.

"Sarah! What the . . . ?"

She stopped because the sourpuss at the front of the room was glaring at her, but she hurried back and sat beside me. "You're going here?" she whispered.

"Yep. I think you're the only person I know in this whole place." My eyes watered.

"Take it easy. I'll introduce you around. I've been at this hell hole since I was like two."

Ann Odom was the wildest girl I knew, but she wasn't a hoodess. She was smart and pretty and rich. Her father was a surgeon. He stitched up Chris's foot once when he stepped on a nail in a neighbor kid's sandbox. Ann had cussed since we were ten or eleven, about the same time she started asking me to duck out of Sunday school to hang out at the drugstore with her. She'd been going steady with an older boy named Bobby Bayne for at least a year; they actually went on car dates.

Maybe there was hope. Just having Ann squire me around till I met some kids might make this penitentiary tolerable.

———•———

Not long after school started, my uncle Draper called to say he and Alice would be passing through Atlanta the following week on their way to Florida. Mother invited them to have lunch—they couldn't stay overnight—and gave them directions to the new house. She and Etha Mae worked every day to get the last boxes unpacked and pictures hung. This time, Mother would not be caught off guard.

By the big day our house looked like it had been lived in for years, and Mother was up, dressed, and arranging flowers when we left for school.

"Enjoy your day," she sang out.

That was the last I saw of her for a couple of days. It seems my uncle called from south of Atlanta to say they were running so late they'd decided to "press on," grab a sandwich to eat on the road. "Maybe" they'd stop on the way home.

The dining room table was still set and the house was dark when I got home. Mother's door was closed and something told me not to knock. Etha Mae would be downstairs ironing. I tiptoed down.

"Didn't my aunt and uncle come by?"

"No, ma'am." Her voice was heavy.

"Where's Mother?"

"Lawd, chil', she went to her room after they called. Said not to disturb her."

Etha Mae didn't mention whether she'd thrown things or run to her room sobbing, and I didn't ask. I was relieved I'd been at school. That night, though, my heart pounded and I couldn't sleep. I felt seasick. I wanted to call my aunt and uncle and tell them to drop dead. My mother had been on a cloud lately, and they'd brought her crashing down.

———•———

Our morning routine changed after the incident with Draper and Alice. Mother stopped getting up to fix breakfast and see us off; my father took over. He would cook eggs and bacon, or set out cereal and fruit on the breakfast room table. He even put a little football-shaped vitamin pill on each of our place mats. All three of us tended to be groggy in the morning, so we ate in silence until Daddy sat down; then he'd chat cheerfully and we'd grunt "un-hunh" or "uh-uh." He didn't complain about having kitchen duty in his starched shirt and business suit.

When we got home in the afternoon, Mother would be staring glassy-eyed at the television or in her room with the door shut. At around five she'd drive Etha Mae to the bus stop, come back, and clank pots and pans in the kitchen. We were not to enter the room between that time and when dinner was served. Forget about getting a piece of fruit or glass of water. If you got five feet from the kitchen door, she screamed, "Get out!"

Annie made a best friend at Howell. Dee lived directly behind us, and in a week or so Annie and Dee had tromped out a path through the woods. They were inseparable, and I was glad because Annie had never had a close friend in our old neighborhood. The first few times Dee came home from school with her, they played Monopoly and giggled in Annie's room, but Mother pounded on the wall from her room. They soon moved to Dee's house, where I imagine they were allowed to talk above a whisper.

Chris made friends fast, so he was off in a flash every day as soon as he dumped his book bag in the back hall, guzzled some Kool Aid, and changed into jeans. I was the only one around to witness Mother's routine. Ann Odom lived too far away to hang out with after school. And she was always with Bobby Bayne anyway. They were supposed to be studying at the library, but she said they usually went to the Varsity for milkshakes or parked at the rock quarry near Howell.

As soon as I changed, I'd go downstairs to talk with Etha Mae. I had spent hours and hours visiting with her in the laundry room at our old house, perched on a tall wooden stool watching her iron. When we weren't talking, she'd sing in her rich alto voice, usually a Negro spiritual or a hymn she'd learned at church. She'd start out humming. "Hmmm, mmm, o-o-oh. Oh, Je-uh-sus, oh, lo-or-ord." From the humming she'd break into a song, almost always about how much she loved Jesus or how he filled her. If you closed your eyes, you would think she was about to cry, her singing was so sad. Actually, she'd have a smile on her face, and she'd sing like she was talking directly to Jesus. Once she got so moved, caught up in singing to him about laying her burden down, she stopped moving the iron. I thought she would singe the shirt, but some holy intervention kept it safe.

"Sometimes I get so full of the Holy Spirit, I almost bust," she said, laughing and crying at the same time. When she finished, she blew her nose, straightened her apron, and went back to ironing.

Mother hated it when Annie or I hung around with Mae. She'd cook up a reason to get us back upstairs as soon as she discovered one of us was down there.

"When we fraternize with hired help, they forget they're employees and the quality of their work plummets," she lectured. "We're all deeply devoted to Etha Mae, but you mustn't fraternize with her."

"What's 'fraternize'?" I asked her, smart-alecky.

"Don't get petulant with me, Sarah. Someday you'll be married and have your own home, and you'll thank me for this instruction. Colored people know their place, and they *want* us to remember ours. It makes them terribly uncomfortable when we don't."

Annie and I ignored her lectures and gossiped with Etha Mae anytime we felt like it. I for one don't think Mother believed a word of her fraternizing speech. I had seen her eating lunch in the kitchen with Mae and talking to her like a friend lots of times.

The laundry room at our new house smelled exactly like the old one, like a mixture of Georgia red clay and bleach and starch. It sounds disgusting, but it smelled *real*. Upstairs there was no odor at all. It was as if our house had been sealed for eternity like a tomb, with trapped gray air hovering in it. The air at Howell was stale and gray too. After suffocating in that atmosphere all day, it was a relief to sit in the cellar with Etha Mae. Her humming and the iron hissing on the damp clothes caused a syrupy feeling in my chest that oozed down into my stomach and out to my arms and legs.

"How you likin' your new school, Miss Sarah?"

"It's gross. The teachers are mean, and the boys are 'high-pock-ets'! Here's how they wear their pants." I hiked my skirt up to my chest and walked with my pelvis stuck out. She threw her head back and howled. I could see gold fillings in the back of her mouth. "Lawd, Miss Sarah, you too much."

"Etha Mae," my mother called from the top of the stairs.

"Yessum?"

"Is Sarah down there?"

"Yessum."

"Well, send her upstairs, please."

Up I went. "What?"

She motioned me into the kitchen. "Don't 'what' me, Sarah. I'm sure you have homework and I want you to do it. Your father's paying a fortune for Howell, and he expects you to apply yourself."

Suddenly it hit me: I was looking her almost directly in the eye, not cowering below the rattlesnake glare. "I'll do it in a little while."

I turned and casually proceeded down the hall and right back down the steps.

"Sarah, come here this instant. You will not put off your homework until after dinner when you're too tired to think!" Her voice rumbled down the stairwell after me, words ricocheting off the bare walls.

I kept going.

CHAPTER 14

Ann Odom was in with the in-crowd at Howell. The wilder you were, the more popular you were. Just the opposite of North Atlanta, where the cheerleaders and athletes were goody-two-shoes and the hoods were wild. Being "in" at Howell meant you drank bourbon and Coke and smoked. You had to make A's but you went wild on the weekends.

It took me a week of choking, shivering, and feeling nauseous to become a smoker. During lunch break every day three or four of us huddled in a bathroom stall and shared a cigarette. We'd pile out reeking of smoke, a blue haze adrift above the stall, wearing I-didn't-do-a-thing-wrong expressions. The nonsmoking, outer circle girls cut their eyes at us, but didn't dare turn us in. They knew our silent treatment—or worse—could ruin their school career.

Joanne Beadle, a quiet, chubby girl, tried to end our tyranny. One day four of us were wedged in a stall, two standing on the toilet and two on the floor, when suddenly a fireball the size of a human head slid under the door and hit the base of the toilet. It was a mass of toilet tissue, which someone had meticulously unrolled, formed into a ball, and lit. We battered one another exiting the stall in a clump, but we made it out alive; Ann Odom beat out the flames with her school blazer. It was a close call, a miracle our clothes hadn't caught fire. Rosa Tanner saw Joanne Beadle hightailing it out of the girls' room about the time of the incident, with guilt written in capital letters on her face.

We couldn't report Joanne, as that would, of course, have gotten *us* in trouble, so we did nothing. But whenever I passed her in the hall, I imagined that she would commit some shocking crime years later.

Ann and her boyfriend, Bobby, wanted to fix me up with a guy named Walt. Bobby and Walt were friends at Northwoods, the public high school near Howell. We would double date to a movie, then go to the Varsity.

"Walt's cute," Ann said. "He looks like Tab Hunter. Well, maybe not *that* cute."

"Yeah, but is he tall?"

"No, Sarah, he's a midget. You'll make a great couple."

"Ann!"

"Yes, he's as tall as you, for crying out loud."

"OK, but I'll have to spend the night with you."

"This table is wrong," Mother announced at dinner one night. "It's unbalanced with five."

Our old dining room table was too small for the new house, so she'd ordered this massive one from North Carolina. It would have looked balanced with the Mormon Tabernacle Choir.

"It's a shame Ben can't enjoy this lovely house," she whined.

"Is Ben coming for my birthday?" Chris asked.

"He probably won't, son, because he has to work," Daddy said.

"No, he won't be coming for your birthday, *or* Annie's birthday, *or* Sarah's birthday," Mother said, her voice quivering. "He's still punishing me." And off she went to the bedroom.

"Is Ben punishing Mama?" Annie asked, a little worry "v" appearing between her eyebrows.

"No, honey," Daddy said. "It's hard for him to get time off."

"I miss him," Annie said.

"Can it! Just can it," I said. "Ben's never coming back. Ever."

I stormed to my room and pulled the door shut hard with both hands, hoping to rock the house. Daddy tapped almost immediately and came in.

"Sally?"

"WHAT?"

"Honey . . ."

"I am *so* sick of Ben this, Ben that. Can't we forget about him?"

He sat on my bed. "Honey, I think Ben will get over this."

"No, Daddy, no! Face it, he's not going to get over it. He told me when I saw him; he's never coming back!"

"He didn't mean that."

"Oh, yes he did. He thinks he's adopted."

"He what?"

"He thinks he's adopted. Are you DEAF?"

He winced. "He's not adopted, Sally."

"That's what I told him!"

Daddy put his head in his hands for a minute and then stared out the window.

"So he's not? He's not adopted?"

"No, honey, of course not."

He limped out like an old man, down the hall—to go check on his blubbering bride, I felt sure.

The blind date was awful. Walt was sixteen and plenty tall, but he was shy and we didn't have much to talk about. He was interested in one thing only—cars—and after he told me how he'd souped up the

'55 Chevy his dad gave him, we were tapped out conversation-wise.

There we sat in the drive-in movie, munching popcorn, pretending nothing out of the ordinary was going on as Ann and Bobby made out in the front seat.

"How'd you like Walt?" Ann asked when we got back to her house. "I couldn't tell."

I shrugged.

"Did you get kissed?"

"No, thank God."

"Whadaya mean, 'thank god'?"

"Ann, this guy kissed me down in New Orleans and . . . it was gross."

"You're joking! He must've done it wrong. Kissing is . . ." She rolled her eyes and swooned. "Is Walt gonna call you?"

"Doubt it."

So much for my first car date. Not only did it *phttt* like a soggy firecracker, it also got me grounded; of course, being grounded isn't punishment when you never do anything to begin with. Mother had called me at Ann's for some lame reason; clearly she was checking on me, so I was caught in my lie.

Our old neighborhood was what you would call "folksy"—people out strolling on the sidewalks, chatting at mailboxes, dropping by with warm cookies. None of that coffee klatch business on our new street. In fact, we lived there several months before either next-door neighbor bothered to introduce themselves.

"They're all snobs," Mother wailed. "And cold. They drive to their mailboxes. Oh, they wave ever so graciously from their Town Cars and Cadillacs, but their push-button windows never come down."

Mother had cut back a lot on her club meetings after the surgery; now week after week she begged off on brass-polishing with the altar guild, and she wouldn't talk to her closest friend, Amelia, on the phone. She stayed locked in her room most days, although sometimes you could hear her splashing in the tub at odd hours, like four in the afternoon. After school we often found her padding around in her robe or her baggy Bermuda shorts. She would roam from room to room as if she were looking for something but had forgotten what it was.

"What's wrong with Mama?" Annie asked Daddy. He'd taken us to Eng's after coming home and finding Mother still in bed, and no sign of any dinner. Daddy studied his plate for a minute, then nudged the fried rice around with his fork.

"She's fine, honey, she just needs to get her mind off herself."

A black sports car roared up our driveway late one Friday afternoon. Most mothers were preparing the evening meal; Catherine Claiborne was not. She was locked in her bedroom. Etha Mae had been forced to hitch a ride to the bus stop with a neighbor. The black car was loud and going too fast. I charged out to wag a finger, Catherine-style, at whoever it was.

Getting out of the car, smiling, was David Blume, a taller, bigger David Blume. I hadn't seen him since the séance.

"How in the world did you find me? What are you doing here? You can drive? Where'd you get this car?"

"Whoa, hold on, could I answer one at a time?"

I laughed. "Sure."

We sat at the wrought iron table on the patio. I didn't want to take him inside. I was still grounded and Mother might say visiting with him was breaking the rules.

"Well, let's see. Laurie told me you moved, and I got the address from information. I called a few times but you were never home."

"Really? Who'd you talk to?"

"Your mom, I guess."

"That car! Where'd you get it? When did you get your license?"

"Slow down, Sarah!"

I laughed again. I wanted to keep laughing. It felt so good to see a familiar face. I'd known David since first grade. He was older, but we had ridden the same school bus.

"I got my license in September . . . on my birthday. They bought me the car a few weeks later."

"Wow. It's neat. What is it?"

"An Austin-Healey. Want a ride?"

"Uh . . . I can't."

"Come on, just around the block."

"David, I'm grounded."

"Still wild, huh? Leading armies of kids around in the dead of night?"

"David, shut up!" I giggled. "You were the one who got bored with the back roads."

We both snickered. I kept looking at him. He looked totally different. "You've changed."

"Braces."

"Huh?"

"The braces are off." He grinned and curled his lips back like My Friend Flicka on TV.

"Oh, yeah, that's it."

I couldn't see what harm it would do to ride around the block with David. It would take five minutes; Mother would never know.

He flopped the convertible top back and off we went, my hair swirling into my eyes and mouth. "I need a scarf!" I screamed over the noise. David's car sounded like a truck, bud-bud-budding down the driveway to the street. "Kinda loud, isn't it?"

"What?"

"Never mind."

I didn't mention David's visit for a while because I didn't see much of Mother; she had become nocturnal. She slept all day, emerging only to prepare dinner, sometimes still in her bathrobe. We ate in silence. Daddy would try to start a conversation with her but get nowhere. She'd check her watch throughout the meal, and as soon as we finished she proceeded to the den.

After I cleared the table Daddy loaded the dishwasher, then joined her; they'd still be in there watching when I went to bed. Annie benefited from Mother's new television obsession because she could babble on the phone with Dee. Chris wasn't bugged about bathing. I guess he put himself to bed—dirty—because it got strangely quiet about ten.

Since Mother was sleeping in the daytime, Etha Mae couldn't get in their bedroom to clean, and often she wasn't sure what she was supposed to do in the house. She did the best she could, though, and was able to keep getting rides to the bus with a neighbor, Mrs. Teal.

"Miss Sarah, remember that time your mama drove us down to see the house she grew up in?" Mae asked one afternoon while I watched her iron.

"Uh, not really, why?"

"Was it in Ansley Park?"

"I don't know; I'm not sure."

"Well, Miz Teal said when she was a little girl Ansley Park was the end of the trolley line. Now the bus comes way out here, Miss Sarah! Miz Teal said this out here was the country back then."

"I remember trolleys," I said.

At dinner I mentioned what Mrs. Teal said about Ansley Park being the edge of civilization back in the good ol' days, and Mother jumped on it like a starved dog on a butcher bone. "Who's Mrs. Teal?"

"The lady across the street. She gives Mae rides to the bus . . . when she takes her maid."

"She lives in the white house?"

"I think so."

Next thing you know, Mother had talked to Mrs. Teal and discovered she was an old school friend. She showed us her picture in the yearbook. Her name was Pauline Nash then. They talked on the phone, Mother visited her, and they went out to lunch together—decked out in hats and gloves. Mother went from flat black to Technicolor overnight. She'd be up and dressed when we got home from school, humming in the kitchen. It was a great time to approach her about David.

"Do you remember David Blume?"

"The name is vaguely familiar."

"He went to Hope School. They lived over on Alder, but then they moved."

"I can't picture him. Is this a contest?"

"No, Mother. May I ride to the North Atlanta sock hop with him? I want to see all my friends."

"You're grounded, remember?"

"It's been a month."

"Oh, has it?"

"Yes."

"Have you had a period?"

"What?"

"You heard me."

"Yes, I'm having it now, Mother. Why?"

She shrugged. "Who knows what you did that night on your clandestine date."

"Mother, for god's sake! That's disgusting."

"Is this a date?"

"What?"

"Are you asking if you can go on a date with David Blume?"

"No, it's not a date. It's a ride to the dance."

"He's Jewish, you know."

"He's Jewish?"

"Sol Blume. His father is Sol Blume. He owns that discount jewelry center over on Cheshire Bridge."

"I thought you didn't *recall* who David Blume was, Mother."

"Well, it came to me, Sarah, and don't sass me."

"So what if David's Jewish?"

"I don't want you dating Jews. You're too young to understand this, but if you married a Jew there would be unimaginable problems. For one thing, the church—"

"I'm not marrying, David, Mother, I'm getting a ride with him!"

I prayed she wouldn't be rude to him when he came to get me, or explode when she realized *he* was driving, not his parents. Fortunately, she wasn't even home on the night of the dance. She and Mrs. Teal had heard about a writers' conference at the University of Georgia in Athens and they went over for the whole weekend.

At first Mother was afraid to go, but Daddy talked her into it. When Mrs. Teal dropped her off that Sunday afternoon, she bustled in, dumped her suitcase, and started jabbering. She'd heard a man named Randall Jarrell do a poetry reading on Friday night, and it was "sooo" good it inspired her; she ended up taking his workshop, even though it was Pauline who was interested in poetry. She'd written six poems, and Randall Jarrell said a number of them were promising and one was very good—publishable! And, oh, she and Pauline had met really interesting people, including this housewife from Valdosta who wrote true crime novels. And who would've thought when you saw this timid little woman that she could interview police and traipse through bloody crime scenes. Yakety-yak.

Other than her excitement about our new house, I don't remember seeing my mother that enthusiastic since "South Pacific," the Broadway musical with Ezio Pinza and Mary Martin, came to the municipal auditorium; she and Daddy had gotten third row seats. She thumbed through a brown pouch she'd bought at the university bookstore and pulled out the poems she'd written. They were mostly about nature—a sunset at Lake Burton, a quiet twilight time by the lighthouse on St. Simon's Island. She had written them in pen but wanted to type them right away, so Daddy lugged the old Remington down from the attic, dusted it, and set it up for her on a card table in the den. She stayed in there clicking away for a week, writing and rewriting, stopping only once to dash over to Mrs. Teal's for her opinion.

It was the best thing that ever happened to me. She was in such high spirits she let me have David Blume over. We hung around outside on the patio at first, but then we came in for a Coke and went downstairs to the playroom. I hauled my hi-fi down there and we listened to records till dinnertime. When he left, she was civilized to him, said "hello" cheerfully and commented on how tall he'd gotten.

After dinner, Annie was clearing the table and called out to

Mother. "Something's going on at your friend's," she said.

Mother and I both went to the dining room; Annie was looking out the window.

"Oh, my god," Mother gasped. "It's an ambulance."

The door of the ambulance was open. Two men in white came out of the Teals', got in the ambulance, and drove up to the back of the Teals' house, out of our sight.

"Oh, my, maybe Pauline's husband had a heart attack . . . or a stroke."

She said Mrs. Teal had invited her and Daddy to come over the next weekend to brunch so they could meet her husband, Bennett. Mother kept watching the Teals' house and grabbing at her throat. Now and then she would release her throat and pick at a little mole underneath her chin. "I don't know whether to call over there. I hate to call in the midst of . . . if it's serious. I wonder what in the world . . ."

CHAPTER 15

*M*other's newfound best friend, Pauline, had dropped dead—suddenly, unexpectedly—of an aneurysm, which my father explained as being like the inner tube in a tire getting weak and pooching out. In this case the inner tube was a blood vessel in Mrs. Teal's brain, and it burst. So my parents met Mr. Teal, but not at the brunch Mother had looked forward to.

After wailing for a day, Mother pulled herself together and baked a ham to take to Mr. Teal. Daddy called it her Woodruff ham because she basted it with bottles and bottles of Coca-Cola. He said the Woodruff family got richer every time she served ham.

"Bennett's in shock," Mother said. "He sits and sits in that armchair and stares while we run around getting things ready. You mark my words, rafts of people are going to descend on that house tomorrow and they'll expect to be fed."

My parents left for the funeral after lunch on Saturday, but Annie, Chris, and I stayed home. We had never attended a funeral, and Mother said she saw no reason for us to go to this one. I had met Mrs. Teal, but other than her, not one person I ever knew died. Well, my grandfather Claiborne died when I was five, but Etha Mae and her sister Grace stayed with Annie and me while my parents went to Savannah.

Annie, on the other hand, had lost her favorite teacher the year before we moved to the new house. Mrs. Mauldin had cancer and taught as long as she could, even in pain, but died before school let out for summer. Some of the children went to the funeral, but Mother wouldn't let Annie go. She said funerals were no place for children. "Ann," she said, "you'll want to remember Mrs. Mauldin with roses in her cheeks, smiling, not sleeping in a box."

Annie began staying in her room reading the King James red-letter edition Bible. She would sit on her bed, flying through the pages, tracing along the lines with her finger, her brow knit. Every day she'd come home and go to her room. "Wouldn't it make you feel better to cry or talk about her?" I asked.

"I don't think so," she said, her eyes unfocused but directed at the Bible page. Her voice sounded like a wise old woman's.

"What are you looking for in there?" I asked her.

She shrugged.

Her reaction seemed strange, but I'd never been where she was right then. After a few weeks, she stopped her ritual and Mother seemed relieved. She had acted perturbed about the whole thing—she, of all people, who would have blubbered and wallowed in misery on a daily basis and expected us to do the same.

When my parents were at Mrs. Teal's funeral, David Blume called. He wondered if I could go to a party with him that night at Kenny Rosenthal's.

"Where does he live?"

"Near you. Don't you remember me taking you over there to see his Vette? Go ask your mom."

"She's at a funeral."

"Well, call me when you find out."

By late afternoon cars had lined up in front of the Teals' house. A lot of young, college-age kids were going up the driveway. Probably friends of the Teals' daughter, who went to college somewhere in Missouri. She was their only child. I wondered how she felt—no brothers or sisters, now no mother.

I showered and decided what to wear that night, then peered out the front window. Most of the cars were gone. I needed to call David back, so I looked up the Teals' number and called.

"Teal residence."

"Excuse me, I'm trying to find Mrs. Claiborne. Catherine Claiborne. Is she still there?"

"Just a minute."

"Hello."

"Mother?"

"What's wrong?"

"Nothing's wrong, but I need to ask you something. May I go to a party with David?"

"Tonight?!"

"Yes, ma'am."

"I cannot believe you. You sit right there."

Click.

The minute she hung up on me and I put down the receiver, the phone rang. It was David.

"She's still not home."

"Oh, well. You're not going to have to eat dinner at home; Kenny bought stuff from the deli. I'll just come on over about seven, OK?"

"Well . . ."

"See you then."

I went ahead and dressed and waited in the den. I thought Mother would be too tired and too sad to argue, and probably glad to have one less kid to cook for. I figured wrong.

"Sarah, you never cease to amaze me. You call me moments after a dear friend's put in the ground to ask about attending a party! Are you feeling FESTIVE?"

Her face was an inch from mine and I could smell liquor. A little spit hit my cheek so I stepped back. "I didn't really know your friend. I don't think it would hurt for me to go to a get-together at someone's house."

She threw down her purse and charged at me, grabbed my throat with both hands and squeezed. I grabbed her wrists and pried her hands off, but it took every bit of my strength. "Daddy!" I screamed.

Mother backed me against the wall, this time pinning my shoulders. "You're a monster."

She wheeled out of the room, nearly mowing down my father. I slumped to a squat, choking, shaking, rubbing my neck.

"Darlin'? Darlin'?" was all Daddy said. He didn't come over to me, just charged out after her. I stood up, wiped my eyes, and ran out the back door. David was turning in when I got to the bottom of our driveway and I held up my hand to stop him there so I could get in.

"Go," I said, looking up at the house, expecting Mother to be charging down the driveway in her new black dress with the epaulets, commanding me to stop. David didn't question me; he just floored it.

Part Four

The smallest worm will turn,
being trodden on.

William Shakespeare, *King Henry IV*

CHAPTER 16

*D*avid called several days after Kenny's party to see how things were going. I told him I didn't know. I hadn't seen Mother in three days. "She's in her room."

"Are you OK?"

"Yeah, I guess. My throat hurts."

"Do you want to do something? Ride around? Go to the Varsity?"

"I need to hang around here for awhile."

"I gotcha. I had fun Saturday."

"Me too."

I had told David what happened when he picked me up for the party. I had no choice; I was so upset. Kenny's parents were out of town, which was why he decided to have people over. I had sneaked into his parents' room and found some makeup to put on the red marks on my neck. David wasn't surprised about what Mother did. He said his father had beaten him with a belt for as long as he could remember. For the littlest things. Like a smart aleck glance.

I didn't tell Ann Odom. I'm not sure why; it's not like her family was hunky-dory. Nobody talked to anybody. Their house was so big you could go about your business and never see another person for days. That's how they lived too, just passing in the halls.

"So when am I going to meet *su hombre*?" Ann asked. She had taken Spanish in middle school and liked to pepper her conversation with Spanish words.

"Huh?"

"Your man."

"Oh, David. I don't know. Maybe I can get him to pick me up after school one day. But you know my mother."

"Tell her you're coming to my house, dummy."

"I can't."

"Listen, Sarah, what your mom doesn't know won't hurt her. *Comprendo*? Do you know what your major maladjustment is?"

"No, Miss Odom, what *is* my major maladjustment?"

"You've never learned the most important skill for every teenager."

"Which is?"

"Zee art of zee leetle white lie."

"The little white lie."

"Didn't you get that talk when you were a kid about it being OK to tell a lie if it kept you from hurting someone's feelings?"

"Yeah."

"For god's sake, Sarah, figure it out!"

David must have been a mind reader. The next day in sixth period I was staring out the window day-dreaming when I spotted his black Austin-Healey in the car pool line. "Ann, I think David's out there."

"Great. Bobby's coming for me and we're going to the rock quarry. Meet us down there."

"I don't know . . . I probably shouldn't."

"Sarah, remember what I told you."

I strolled down the line of cars to my friend Rosa's mother's station wagon. She'd already been by the lower school and the middle school because Chris and Annie were in the backseat.

"Hi, Mrs. Tanner. I'm not riding today. I've got to go to Ann Odom's to study."

"All right, dear. Does your mother know?"

"I'll call her." I looked at Annie. "Tell Etha Mae, OK?"

Annie shot me a grave look, like I'd asked her to hold up a Brinks truck. "Sure," she said, and stuck her nose back in the book she was reading.

I continued walking down the line till I got to the black sports car. It was David, but I didn't stop. "Meet me behind the gym," I said out of the corner of my mouth. Then I cut behind his car and crossed the bridge over the pond that separated the upper school and administration building from the area of campus with the cafeteria, chapel, and fine arts building. The gym was in the woods beyond. I strode like I had a purpose, hoping not to run into a teacher, or worse, our headmaster.

David was waiting for me, grinning. "Hop in."

"Mother's going to kill me."

"Let's go to the library and you can call."

"No, I'm not calling. We're meeting my friend Ann and her boyfriend at the rock quarry."

Ann and Bobby were parked at the edge of a steep cliff. Too close to the edge, David said. He pulled over and stopped about four car lengths behind them. When we got up to Bobby's car, I saw the famous rock quarry for the first time. It was a deep bowl with craggy sides like a miniature Grand Canyon. At the bottom was a lake with ink-black water, smooth as glass. The afternoon sun flicked silver sparks across it.

"Come to watch the submarine races with us?" Bobby laughed.

David chuckled. I didn't get it.

I introduced David to Ann and Bobby. Bobby wanted to see David's car, so they walked back and started looking under the hood. I got in the driver's seat of Bobby's car to talk with Ann. She immediately pulled a beer from a little cooler between her feet and held it out to me.

"No, thanks."

"Come on, Sarah."

"They'll smell it when I get home."

"I've got Clorets for that. Here."

When he got back over to us, David took a beer too. "Let's explore," he said, looking at Ann and Bobby.

"Nah, we've seen it all," Bobby said.

David and I hadn't, so we roamed off down a path to see if it went to the bottom. It didn't, but it led to an outcropping about halfway down the quarry wall. You could tell that kids came here from the beer cans and Coke bottles, and a blackened pit where they'd had campfires. David and I sat on a smooth boulder and looked out over the lake.

"This beer is gross," I said.

"I like it. Nice and cold."

We sat there not saying anything and then I stood up and started dropping pebbles, waiting, then hearing them plunk in the water below. I wanted to enjoy myself, but I kept thinking about walking in our back door and facing my mother, maybe getting choked again.

David came up behind me and put his arms around my waist. I froze. It was exactly like Russell had done at my brother's, but there was no mirror, just a cliff that would kill you if you went over the side.

"What are you doing?" I asked, my voice wavery.

He let go of me and walked over and got a rock and tossed it out.

He looked like a little kid with his hair falling down over his fore-head. In the sun it had blond streaks on top. I ran over and grabbed his arm. "I'm throwing you over," I said in a menacing tone. "No one will ever find you."

He reached in his pocket and shook his keys at me. "And you'll be the proud owner of a 1960 Austin-Healey."

I grabbed the keys and ran up the path. I could hear him close on my heels. When he grabbed the back of my blouse, I squealed and turned to face him.

"I've got you now."

"So?" I said, and gave him a smug look.

"So you're my prisoner, Miss Wild Thing."

At that point I was leaning against a tree looking up at him, smil-ing and panting from our chase up the hill. He leaned down and kissed me on the lips. Gently. His lips were soft and I closed my eyes. Then he brushed his face across my cheek and rested his head next to mine for a minute. I could hear him breathing. "Beat you to the car," he whispered and we tore off up the path.

I had David drop me off at our corner, in case Mother was watching for me out the window. Fortunately, she hadn't emerged from her bedroom to start dinner, so I slipped into my room, put on a stack of 45s, and flopped on my bed face-first.

The mountain's high and the valley's so deep,
Can't get across to the other side . . .

I lay there listening to the words, thinking about the quarry. I wanted to go back out there with David. I wanted him to kiss me exactly the way he had today. Every day. I closed my eyes and played out the scene in my head. I could still feel his lips; I swallowed hard.

The next record didn't drop and "The Mountain's High" started playing again. I was trying to fix it when my door flew open. "You weren't at the Odoms," Mother said.

"I know."

"Where were you?"

"The library."

I continued restacking records.

"Why did you lie to Scotti?"

"Who?"

"Mrs. Tanner."

"I didn't lie. I *was* going to Ann's, but the plan changed. I rode with a girl from Latin to the library. We studied, then she brought me home."

"Why didn't you call?"

"I didn't want to wake anybody up, anybody who *might* be sleeping in the middle of the afternoon."

I stood facing her within arm's reach, so I steeled myself to be slapped or strangled—whatever. She looked floored that I would speak to her in such a tone.

"That was thoughtful of you, Sarah." She turned to leave. Peacefully. Now it was my turn to be dismayed. Maybe Ann Odom was right. Maybe lying was the key. The secret to freedom. Then Mother turned and smiled at me. "Dinner at seven," she said in a honey-dipped voice.

I just looked at her.

"And Sarah, brush those pine needles off the back of your skirt before you hang it up, would you, dear?"

———•———

"Who decided on these atrocious uniforms?" I asked Ann. I'd gone home with her after school.

"We've had these colors for as long as I can remember. You think *you're* sick of 'em."

For girls at Howell the winter uniform was a gray skirt, white blouse, and dark wine-colored blazer with the school crest on the pocket. Not my colors. I looked especially sickly in white. "If I could just throw on a madras belt or some other color top for a change."

"Sarah, we need to do makeup on you!"

"No way."

"Why do you never wear a lick of makeup?"

"Uh, Catherine Claiborne. Remember her?"

"Well, Sarah, she can't control what you do when you're out of sight. Now, c'mon, sit down right here."

I couldn't believe my eyes when Ann finished with me. And it was so simple—a little rouge on my cheek bones, brown mascara, and lipstick. She also plucked my eyebrows to give them an arch; it was torture. I sneezed between every pluck and my mascara ran, so we had to cold cream my cheeks and re-do the rouge and mascara.

"I should've done your damn eyebrows first. Now let's see about this hair."

"What's wrong with my hair?"

"Shush, would ya?"

Ann back-combed every hair on my head and then tried to smooth out the wildness with a brush. "I look like I've been electro-cuted."

"Hmm . . . well, yeah, you're right. Let's start over."

She brushed out all the knots and I "ouched" while she cussed. But it was worth it. On the second try she changed my part, which played up my widow's peak.

"Woo! You look sexy. David's gonna fall in love. Wait, one more thing. Try this on."

"Why?"

"Go in the bathroom, Sarah, put this on, and then come right back out."

It was a lacy bra with wires on the bottom and little half-moon pads stuffed into the sides. I stuck my head out. "I don't need a 'cheater' bra, Ann."

"Put it on," she shrieked. "This too." She tossed me a pale blue cashmere sweater.

You don't argue with Ann; it's not worth it. And, you know, I was floored when I looked in the long mirror on the back of her closet. It wasn't me standing there; I don't know who it was.

When I got home Mother called me a slut, which I had to look up in the dictionary. I'd rubbed off most of the rouge and blotted my lips, so I wasn't drastic in any way. But when I walked in, she called me to the den and looked me up and down. Her expression didn't change. She took a big sip of whatever liquid was sloshing around with ice cubes in her orange Tupperware glass. Then she said in a flat voice, "Slut." I pivoted and strolled back to my room nonchalantly, but my heart was pounding. I waited for her to blast through the door and sling a jar of cold cream at me, demand that I take off the makeup, but she never came.

I debated about washing my face and combing my hair back to the old way, but decided to leave it. Daddy squinted at me as though he noticed something different, but didn't mention it. He was edgy because Mother had put our dinner on the table and then gone to bed without eating. It was just Chris and me and Daddy at the table; Annie was spending the night at Dee's.

"Is Mommy sick?" Chris asked suddenly, and Daddy stopped

chewing mid-bite. This was new. Chris was usually in his own little world of touch football and tree houses and didn't notice Mother's behavior. Daddy didn't answer.

"Can I try her typewriter?"

"Son, I think she's working on something. Maybe you'd better not."

"She isn't using it!"

"Hey, Chris, I've got something neat to show you after dinner," I said. I hoped the diagram of frog dissection in my biology book would distract him. God knows what would happen if Mother heard him thumping on her Remington, even though she hadn't touched it since Mrs. Teal died.

She stayed in bed all weekend. Our house was morgue-like with the shutters and curtains closed, and Daddy kept asking us to be quiet. The hush-hush was maddening. That was nothing new, but something in the air felt different this time. My father was taking her meals on a tray, but she wasn't eating. Maybe this time she was really sick.

CHAPTER 17

When we got home from school on Monday, Etha Mae was sitting at the kitchen table sniffling, dabbing her nose with a big white handkerchief. "Yo mama is so put out with me," she said.

Chris drank some Kool-Aid and tore off to his room. Annie didn't even stop to say hello to Mae. She never hung around if there was trouble in the air, even if it meant skipping her after-school snack. Come to think of it, she wasn't eating constantly now. Maybe Dee was a good influence; she was broom-straw thin.

"Etha Mae, my mother has been mad at everybody since Ben left. And . . . the cancer . . . look, she's not angry at you." I patted her shoulder. "She just takes stuff out on you."

At that, she cried harder. "She's gone, Miss Sarah. Gone to some hospital."

"What happened?"

"Lawd have mercy, I don't know. She got dressed in her nice black suit and left out of here with a little suitcase. Not a hello or good-bye. I called yo daddy . . . and then she called me and fussed 'cause I called him . . . and now he's comin' home."

"Slow down, Mae," I said, sitting down beside her. "So she's in the hospital?'

She blew her nose and kept blubbering. "She tol' me to min' my own business, Miss Sarah."

My father walked in, gray-looking, hair flopped down over his glasses.

I stood up. "What's going on?" I asked him.

"Honey, listen for the phone; your mother may call. I need to take Mae now or she'll miss the last bus."

"You need me to stay, Mister Claiborne?"

"No, Mae, but thank you."

"Daddy, please!"

"Your mother's all right, Sally. I'll explain as soon as . . . I'll be back in ten minutes."

When he got home he gathered all three of us in the study and informed us that mother had checked herself into a "special" hospital. "She got so sad after Pauline . . . after Mrs. Teal across the street died. Er, your mother was so blue she felt frightened."

"About what, Daddy?" Annie asked.

"She was very upset, so she called Jim Breen, Dr. Breen, up the street, and he thought she should go rest—just for a while—at his hospital."

"Dr. Breen owns a hospital?" I said.

"It's a small hospital where she can get a lot of good rest. Don't you children worry; she'll be home in no time."

My father would've said that if Mother had been mowed down by a cement mixer and was lying in pieces. Annie was beginning to catch on to Daddy's blue-sky version of things too; she started to cry. Chris sat in the big leather arm chair, wriggling, but stone-faced. "Can I go outside?" he asked.

"All right, son, but don't go far; we're going out to dinner."

Maybe Mother will get fixed at this "special" place, I thought, change the two records she plays over and over—"sad and sobbing," and "mad and screaming." Granted, she had played one other happy song about the new house and the poetry writing, but not for long. I wanted a mother like everybody else had. Maybe one like Wendy's.

So I was relieved in a way, hopeful that this "rest" was going to help. Until I went to Breen. Daddy wasn't sure Chris and Annie were old enough to be allowed in, so they didn't go that first time. Thank god, because it wasn't a cozy little rest haven; it was a nuthouse.

The place itself was beautiful, like Tara in *Gone with the Wind,* a mansion on a hill with emerald green grass surrounding it. But Prissy and Scarlett weren't there. Instead, totally crazy people were everywhere—rocking on the big front porch, their eyes glazed over; shuffling in the halls like sleepwalkers; yowling dirty words from locked rooms with little square windows in the doors.

I tried not to stare, but I couldn't help sneaking looks, like when you discover a hole in your tooth where a filling has come out, and you poke your tongue in it over and over. You know the hole isn't supposed to be there, and you'll have to tell someone, and you'll be forced to go to the dentist and have it drilled on. But you keep hoping you'll stick your tongue back there and—miraculously!—the hole will be gone. In the same way, I kept glancing at the people in that place, hoping to see someone who was nicely dressed, someone who looked normal. But only nasty, messy weirdos were rocking and drooling, or hovering around. With *my mother.* The dignified Southern lady who could click into a room in her high heels and Leon Froshin's outfit, lift one eyebrow and have everyone kowtowing to her. The lady who won blue ribbons and silver bowl trophies for her flower arrangements, who could transform a dirt pile into "Yard of the Month," write a poem on her first try that the famous Mr. Jarrell raved about.

I thought about running back to the car and rolling up in a ball. Instead, I did the exact same thing my idiotic father did in gruesome situations—grinned and acted as though I were at a fair or carnival, maybe a prom, somewhere fun. Having a fine time. Lovely. Would I like a Coca-Cola? Sure, that would be nice. Charming. My mother is here in a loony bin and we're sipping Coke and making small talk.

I hated Ben. This was his fault. Yeah, Mother'd been bossy and pitched fits now and then before he left, but his leaving and refusing to speak to her shoved her right over the edge. Before we even got to her room, I decided to go home and write him, tell him what it was like having your mother locked up in an insane asylum, and that I hoped he was enjoying himself in the French Quarter watching the bus named "Desire" truck up and down in front of his cool beatnik pad.

Mother was playing a brand new tune that day at Breen. She spoke in hushed tones and acted like a polite child. Maybe she had to put on this show. Maybe they beat you if you didn't behave. "Hey, sweetie pie," she said and pecked me on the cheek. She smelled like baby powder.

She didn't say anything to Daddy, just took the bags of clothes from him that we'd stopped and gotten at Rich's. She pulled the dresses out and laid them out on the bed one at a time. "Oh, these are good. Look, they put me in these." She frowned down at the khaki pants that were too big and looked like a man's, and the pink cotton camp shirt, not tucked in. "Sally, honey, I do need some shoes. These slippers are awful. Could you bring my navy flats when you come tomorrow?"

She seemed weak and confused. While we sat there searching for something to say, a little old lady who looked like Mamie Eisenhower drifted in and started arranging things on the dresser. She lined up Mother's comb, brush, and glasses case in a perfectly straight row. I braced myself for Mother to yell at her to get out. Instead, she smiled and shrugged. "Poor old soul, she comes by and fiddles with those things every few hours."

This could not be my mother. I had no idea what to say to this person. "How's the food?" "What do you do for fun?" What do people talk about in a mental institution? Daddy made ridiculous comments in baby talk, like "Look at your nice view, darlin'," and nodded toward her barred window.

After she toured us through her wing—to the lounge, the crafts and recreation room, the group therapy room—there was nothing else to do. We said good-bye. "I'll be home soon," she whispered. "It's depressing being around all these sick people."

My bitchy grandmother arrived two days later on a train from Savannah; she was afraid to fly. Gram loved a crisis. She hadn't visited us in five years, not since Mother had to go to Charleston for her grandfather's funeral. Daddy had stayed home because my leg was in a cast and Chris had chicken pox. Gram thought Daddy needed her help, but her coming only added to his problems; she's very demanding.

I put off going home after school to avoid her. David came to pick me up and we went out to the rock quarry.

"Aren't you bringing a book?" David asked as we got out of his car.

"I've been looking at books all day. I'd rather look at the sky."

"Well, can you carry mine while I get the food and the blanket?"

"No, I'm too weak," I said, fluttering my eyelashes.

David laughed and jabbed the book at me. Fortunately it was exam time, so no other kids were around. We went down past the place where we'd first kissed to a clearing that had a grassy area over-looking the water, and a rock ledge that jutted out.

"I told Etha Mae I was having dinner at Ann Odom's. Where are you supposed to be?"

"I don't have to be as specific as you do. I just tell my mother when I'll be home."

"I hate you!"

"She wasn't always like this. She eased off for some reason after I got my car."

We spread out the blanket and David opened his book, *The Oxford Book of American Verse.*

Is that for English?"

"No, it's for me."

"You're kidding! I hate poetry. I never understand what they're trying to say."

"Well, you've got to give it some time. You can read a poem five or six times before you catch the meaning. Then you go, 'aha, I get it,' you know?"

"Show me one you went 'aha' with."

"Let's see."

He flipped pages while I stared at him. Amazing. Here was this big guy who played basketball, fixed cars, could read Hebrew, *and* appreciate poetry. I leaned against his arm as he stopped on a T. S. Eliot poem, "The Love Song of J. Alfred Prufrock."

"Here's one of my favorites.

Let us go then, you and I,
When the evening is spread out against the sky
Like a patient etherised upon a table;
Let us go, through certain half-deserted streets,
The muttering retreats
Of restless nights in one-night cheap hotels
And sawdust restaurants with oyster shells:
Streets that follow like a tedious argument
Of insidious intent

To lead you to an overwhelming question . . .
Oh, do not ask, 'What is it?'
Let us go and make our visit.

"What do you think?"

"It's OK."

"Listen to this:

I should have been a pair of ragged claws
Scuttling across the floors of silent seas."

"He wants to be a crab?"

"Well, I finally decided—after reading it over and over—he was depressed about getting old. But you can tell he loved life."

"Umm."

"And he knew he had to go on. I mean, he wasn't suicidal."

"How do you know?"

"Well, here, where he says, 'Do not ask' . . . that part. I think he's saying not to question life, just live it.'"

"I don't want to read something a billion times to get it. I like writers who come right out and say what they mean. Like . . . go back to that part . . . what was that thing about the patient?"

"'When the evening is spread out against the sky like a patient etherised . . .' Oh, he's depressed, so the sky looks flat and dull to him."

"I'd rather have a flat sky overhead than be in my house with the ceilings closing down on me. Any sky would be better."

David read on to himself; I lay there thinking about how much I didn't want to go home. Gram had taken over my room and I had to move into Annie's room; no privacy for me while Mother made potholders out at Breen. Plus, we'd be eating Gram's cooking, and she overcooked everything.

Finally David closed his book, leaned down and kissed me. It was a soft kiss that I wanted to last forever, but he stopped after a few minutes and looked at me. "You could try smiling."

I burst into tears. He pulled back and I sat up, humiliated. I had no warning I was going to cry, but tears spurted out.

"I'm sorry," David said.

"No, it wasn't you, David." I poured out the Breen story, including gory details of the place and my mother acting so pitiful. I told him about overhearing Daddy telling Gram that what had scared Mother into going there was thoughts of suicide. I told it all, knowing he wouldn't want anything to do with me after hearing it.

"I've been out there," he said.

I caught my breath. "To Breen?"

"I wasn't a patient! My aunt went there to dry out."

"Dry out?"

"Alcoholics go out there to stop drinking. It's pretty bleak. I hated visiting her. I only went that one time."

"I don't want Chris and Annie to go."

"Tell your dad."

"David, if Mother wants them to come, he won't have any say in the matter."

When my grandmother first arrived I had toured her around the house. It was the first time she'd seen it, but she never showed any expression or made any comments about anything—until we got to my parents' bedroom. There, her eyebrows shot up. "Twin beds!"

I shrugged and she made a clucking noise with her tongue. In the living room, she sat on the first chair she reached and waved at the piano. "Play something for me, please, Sarah."

"Gram, I stopped taking lessons when I was twelve."

"Go ahead, dear. Can you play 'Beautiful Dreamer'? I love that piece."

"I don't know that one." I was flipping through music books in the piano bench. She nagged until I dug out tattered sheet music for *Porgy and Bess*. I struggled through "Summertime" and she sucked her teeth on every wrong note. "You must practice, dear," she said at the end.

"Gram? Why did you get a beach house for Draper and Alice but not us?" She fidgeted with her pearl necklace and looked at her feet. "It was two summers ago. Uncle Bob and Aunt Bet were invited too. But not us!"

Gram's eyes darted around the room.

"It kind of hurt my feelings."

"Well, it shouldn't have," she snapped. "I've found it's better to visit with my sons—and their wives—individually."

"But why? Why can't we all come to Savannah like we used to? Come over and go out to the beach."

"If you must know, there's tension . . . it's jealousy, if you ask me. I don't want to be bothered with it." She clamped her lips together.

"Who's jealous?"

"They all are. Alice is jealous of your mother's education. Bob begrudges your father's success. Catherine gets upset when I give anything to Draper or Bob. There was a scene over a mantle clock, I recall."

"What's Daddy jealous about?"

"I cannot imagine. But I'm sure he is. They all are."

I dropped it, wondering if my grandmother wasn't jealous of us. She'd refused to compliment our house, a house that was much nicer than hers in Savannah.

CHAPTER 18

*M*other checked herself out of Breen after two weeks. She said everyone there was crazy but her, and the staff were all stupid. If she'd left one day earlier, Chris and Annie wouldn't have had to go, but on Sunday we went for afternoon visiting hours. Gram stayed home.

Right away, Chris saw a kid on the front porch fooling with baseball cards and ran over to him. I kept an eye on him while Daddy and Annie went to get Mother. When they came out, Annie was clutching her stomach like someone had kicked her.

Daddy found an empty chair at the end of the porch—off, away from everyone—and seated Mother there. We circled in front like subjects before their queen.

"Surely these people could think of more creative projects," she said. "I have nothing to show for hours in that recreation room but a crocheted tissue box cover and a few tacky potholders. And this horrid habit." She was smoking. "Edward, is your mother going through our drawers?"

Daddy looked puzzled.

"Never mind. I'll know the moment I get home if anything's out of place. When is she leaving?" She didn't wait for an answer. "I tell you, I could help these people more than the so-called doctors out here. I'm going to write Jim Breen a long report. You can't imagine what I've seen!"

On and on she ranted. Everyone around us moved away, or scattered to the *Gone With the Wind* front lawn. Chris and Annie took over two chairs that had been vacated nearby. When I saw them rocking, my arm hairs stood up. It was the exact picture the gypsy in New Orleans had described. I'd thought the woman was a fake, but she'd seen this! Did she know my mother was going to a nuthouse? If she saw it in her tea leaves, why didn't she warn me?

Mother wasn't transformed into the mother I wanted, but in a way it was a relief to find her more like she'd always been. Annie and Chris didn't have to witness the timid little fraidy-cat I had seen on that first visit.

Gram left the day after Mother got home, thank the lord. She had stunk up my room with rose water, and a thin film of her talcum powder covered every surface in my bathroom. She was a witch. The last thing out of her mouth was a question about Ben, when was he coming home. She knew the story on Ben, and her question was *meant* to upset my mother. I wanted to rip her gray hair out of her ancient silver combs. Mother didn't act surprised; she seemed to expect Gram to broadside her.

"He's too busy with his new job to leave just now, but we're going down for Thanksgiving. Won't that be lovely?"

"Lovely," Gram said, but she pursed her lips. She knew she'd been one-upped.

After Gram left, Mother made a new friend, Black and White scotch. She'd look across the street at the Teals' house, then head for the liquor cabinet. Even when she was sipping from a Tupperware tumbler at four in the afternoon, at a time when most people were having Coke or tea, you could tell it was liquor because of the rattlesnake look in her eyes, especially the left one, which her bifocal reading glasses magnified on the bottom.

"We're going to have Thanksgiving with your brother this year," Mother announced at dinner.

"Yea!" Chris clapped and reared back in his chair.

Annie beamed.

"What does Ben say about this?" I asked.

"He doesn't know, Sarah. We're going to surprise him. And don't you dare spoil this by writing him."

"It's a long drive," I said, my heart racing.

"We're not driving. We're taking the train."

"I've never been on a train," Annie said.

"You're going to love it. I got us three Pullman compartments. We'll sleep on the train."

"I'm not going, Mother. I've been and I'm not going again."

"Well, you're going, like it or not."

I didn't go and I didn't warn Ben. It was his problem. When Mother was in Breen, I chickened out about writing him a nasty letter. He'd balled her up like a used paper napkin and thrown her away; he could do that to me too. Instead, I wrote a newsy letter and tossed in nonchalantly where Mother was—an "oh, by the way, Mother's in a nuthouse" kind of thing. He never even bothered to call to check on her. I wasn't going to write him for a long time. Let him be bowled over when they all showed up at his slum.

Fortunately, I was able to stay with Ann Odom. One more person in their house was no big deal. David and I were going to the Georgia Tech–Georgia freshmen football game, which was always on Thanksgiving weekend. We were discussing our plans a few days before, and David started acting weird. "Sarah, I've got to ask you a favor," he said. His voice was thick.

"Uh . . . look, if we run into any of my parents' friends at the game, I've got to introduce you as somebody else. We've got to come up with a different name for you."

"What are you talking about?"

"I haven't told you this before; I didn't want to upset you. My parents are pretty religious. They're Orthodox. They'd ground me in a minute if they caught me with a Gentile girl."

My eyes watered. "Oh. So you've been sneaking out with me this whole time?"

"Sarah, I—"

"Why don't you tell them I'm just a friend?"

"Do you want me to lose my car?"

Mother's brilliant idea to surprise Ben was a giant bust. He'd gone to Texas with Russell, so my family ate their turkey dinner alone in a restaurant, a bad one Mother read about in a tourist guide. I tried to get details from Annie, but she kept talking about the train, and the neat little pull-down beds, and their Mississippi riverboat ride. I was glad she'd had fun. "I didn't get to do that when I went down," I said. "We didn't have time."

"Ben's apartment looked crummy," Annie said.

"You went there?"

She nodded.

"Did Mother flip?"

She shrugged. She said she was disappointed that she didn't get to see Ben. She *said*. I don't think she meant it. I believe she'd forgotten him. It was hard for me to remember how he looked after only six months.

Annie snickered. "Chris saw some ladies with their tops off."

"Where?"

"Through a door. We were riding down Bourbon Street. He said, 'Wow-wee!'"

Imagining it, I had to laugh.

My holiday had fallen as flat as theirs. I was panicked throughout the football game because, of course, we bumped into the Blumes' close friends. I was introduced as Sarah Stein. David had a high old time, while I sat worried that the Roths would ask why they'd never seen me at the temple. If that wasn't enough, in the traffic jam after the game, David saw somebody else his parents knew, and he made me duck down.

Ann Odom insisted I break up with him.

"Ann, it's not David. It's his parents. Saying I was Sarah Stein was a white lie. Remember your advice? To lie? 'Zee leetle white lie,' you called it."

"No way I'd be hiding on floorboards."

"But I really like him. We went over to my house after the game."

"Did you go all the way?"

"Ann!"

"Well, did you make out at least?"

"Quit interrupting. Yes, as a matter of fact! We'd only kissed a few times before, but this was more. We kissed for about an hour, and then he tried to unbutton my blouse."

"So?"

"So I said no."

"What'd he say?"

"He said he really cares about me."

"It's gonna get worse. Bobby gets so hot he starts begging."

"For what?"

"To do it, you idiot! Screw!"

"And . . . do you let him?"

"No! I don't care to end up at that unwed mothers' place down in Jonesboro."

"So?"

"So I help him out."

I was in shock. I couldn't sleep that night after Ann told me how she relieved Bobby's "painful pressure"—into a Dixie cup, no less.

CHAPTER 19

That Mother didn't end up back at Breen after the fiasco in New Orleans was a miracle. I'd thought she would at least take to her bed, but a "project"—at church, of all things—derailed her depression train. Suddenly, she was on a new mission that had more to do with me than Ben for a change. She was busily rounding up stuff to sell in the church's Christmas bazaar; she seemed to forget about her old friend, Black & White scotch.

One morning she was acting palsy-walsy with me, asked real chatty if I'd been drawing lately. I told her no. "Do you still have that sketch of your brother's apartment?"

"I'm not sure."

"Could you look?"

I wondered what she was up to, but dug it out.

"May I keep this?"

"Why?"

"For the bazaar. I'll have Millen's frame it."

"You're giving it away?"

"Sarah, please, honey . . . everyone in the church circle has to donate ten items."

"Nobody's gonna want that."

"Oh, you'd be surprised. A framed New Orleans scene? Please think about it. It's for a good cause."

"What's the good cause, building a *bigger* cathedral?"

"Lower your voice, please. All proceeds go to Samaritan House this year. We ought to give something, if small, to those who have nothing."

"Where is everybody?" I asked my friend Rosa.

"Who knows? Probably cramming for Warner's test." Smoke haloed her head. We were in a stall in the girls' restroom. Rosa was perched on one side of the commode; I was sitting on the floor with my feet stuck out into the next stall.

Mr. Warner had systematically terrorized us for two weeks about the exam, but I couldn't study anymore. I'd gone over my notes until a hundred years of important events had blurred together. "I detest American history."

"It's not history, Sarah; it's memorizing dates. I couldn't care less."

Somebody walked in and Rosa squinted through the crack to see who it was. She shrugged, so I knew it wasn't Joanne Beadle coming to torch us again. "Who're you taking to Ann's party?" she asked me.

"Me, myself, and I."

"How 'bout that guy David?"

"He wouldn't know anybody."

"I'm scared. Pete and I are staying all night, and if his parents find out—if *my* mother finds out—we're fried."

"I'm spending the night too. I have to; my curfew's ten-thirty and people won't even get there till eight-thirty or so."

"You're kidding. You have to be home at ten-thirty?"

"Yep, my mother thinks I'm still two."

Ann Odom's parents were going to Colorado to ski. Her aunt was coming from South Carolina to stay with her and her brothers, but she wasn't getting there until Sunday afternoon. Ann and I were to babysit on Saturday night, and Ann got the idea to have a party. It was getting out of control; thirty or so kids were coming for sure.

"I don't see why you won't ask David," Ann said. "Y'all can have my bed. Bobby and I've got dibs on my parents'."

"I don't want to sleep with David."

"You don't have to *do it,* for Pete's sake. You could just snuggle. Wouldn't you like to curl up all night in his arms?"

"Not really." Things had progressed with David exactly the way Ann predicted. The more we made out, the farther he wanted to go. "Five minutes after we start kissing, he's like a stranger, some totally different person."

"I know, they start groaning and get this glazed look in their eyes."

No way was I getting in bed with David and going through our usual discussing and arguing for a whole night. "Last time we were at the quarry he got furious."

"How come?"

"I wouldn't let him unhook my bra."

"Why not?"

"Ann! His parents think Gentiles are trash, remember? Do you want me to *be* trash?"

"Ple-uzz!! His parents weren't in the back seat!"

"Oh, and every time I get home with my lipstick smeared, Mother calls me a tramp. No way I'm turning into a whore and prove her right. I'm holding out just to spite her."

———•———

Daddy drove me to Ann's on Saturday morning. She needed help getting ready for the party. As soon as my father turned out of the driveway, we set off on foot for Country Corner, a convenience store four streets over. It took both of us to haul the bags back to her house: chips, dips, pretzels, Coke, ginger ale. After Ann put the food away, we collected the breakable knickknacks in the den and stored them up high in closets.

"We'll pretty much be in here," Ann said. "I don't want to take any chances. Mother would croak if one of her *precious* vases got smashed. Or this." She lifted a large oval plate from its stand on the bookcase. "Imari. Very expensive."

Bobby Baynes showed up after lunch and hulked on the sofa watching TV while we spread pimento cheese on Ritz crackers and baked two pans of brownies. During a commercial he went out to his car and came back with a brown bag. "Hide this somewhere, babe. It's just for us."

Ann peered into the bag. "Woo! How'd you get this?" She slid the bottle out to show me. Bourbon.

"My parents got a case for the holidays. Jack in the black. They won't miss *one*, huh?" He laughed like a honking goose. I couldn't see what Ann saw in him, although he was handsome in a greasy Elvis kind of way. He wasn't very smart. He'd failed a grade in grammar school, so he was seventeen and only a junior.

"Bobby, how 'bout disappearing so Sarah and I can get ready? We need to primp."

"Huh?"

"Why don't you come back about six and we'll go get a hamburger?"

He whimpered like a kicked mutt, but she kissed him and he left like he was told.

I used Ann's bathroom and she used her parents' to shower and shampoo. While she piled on makeup, I sat under her dryer, and then we switched. Fortunately, she'd packed her brothers off to spend the night with friends, so we had the house to ourselves.

"Am I the only one without a date?"

"Nah. Bobby asked some guys from Grady. Football players."

"I meant girls."

Oh, Jennifer's coming. You know her, that senior who comes in and smokes with us. The wild one that looks like a goody-goody."

The party was a horror show. Bobby's jock friends swept in with coolers of beer and whiskey they'd filched from their parents, and they proceeded to get gross and rowdy. The couples from Howell fled to various bedrooms and never came out. I didn't see Bobby and Ann after about ten o'clock. The football animals smoked cigars and butted them out in house plants. One guy closed a brownie in one of Dr. Odom's medical books and filed it back on the shelf. Most of the night, Jennifer and I danced with Rick Burch and Taylor somebody from Howell; then some jerk pawed at Jennifer, and Rick shoved him into a lamp, which crashed to the floor. Turns out it was OK except for the shade holder being cockeyed.

I knocked on Ann's parents' door hoping I could get Bobby to make his friends go home. No answer. How could they sleep with the noise? And wasn't Ann concerned about her house?

Finally the animals passed out, and Jennifer and I went to Ann's bedroom; I locked the door and propped a chair under the knob. I'd had about thirty minutes of sleep when the sound of Jennifer barfing woke me up. She needed help because she was out of her head. "Burboo mus' not agree with . . ." She pitched forward over the bowl again, swaying on her knees. I held her hand and swabbed her brow for hours, until she was able to crawl back to bed around sunup. Not long after that, Ann pounded on the door.

I removed my barricade and unlocked it. "What is it?"

"We've got about four hours to fix this place before my aunt comes. You're my only hope. You gotta help me."

I felt sick from no sleep, but every bed in Ann's house needed to be stripped. There was vomit—and other unidentifiable stains—on sheets, spreads, even rugs. Plants were overturned and the kitchen was a disaster. I ran the washer and dryer, load after load, and remade beds while Ann hauled out bags of trash, righted furniture, and vacuumed. We added water to the half-empty bottles in her parents' liquor closet, which one of the jocks had jimmied the lock on. I carefully Scotch taped fractured limbs on plants in the den and living room.

"There's a cigarette hole in this leaf," I called out to Ann.

"Cut it off," she hollered back.

We plied Jennifer with coffee and sent her on her green-faced way. Everyone else had cleared out before Ann woke me up. Except for a tiny nick on the refrigerator, all was ship-shape by the time Daddy tooted for me. Ann hugged me as I left. "You saved my life."

Our house became the staging center for the church bazaar. Twenty-three Westchester Circle was at the bull's-eye of the St. Martha's Guild membership, so all the ladies were bringing their donations to our house to store in our playroom. After everything was gathered, the sexton from the cathedral would come in a truck to collect it. Every day somebody's husband lugged something in—a hall tree, a carton of antique Christmas ornaments, a soup tureen. Mother commented on each item. "That's Wedgewood!" she shrieked. "How can Lillian part with it?" She felt outdone. She had donated a gilt picture frame and a Victorian mirror she'd never liked; the rest was junk, or so she thought until the biddies raved about my New Orleans slum scene.

"They want more, Sarah. They'd like you to do more drawings, but they think pen-and-inks would sell better."

"What's a pen-and-ink?"

"All you have to do is a pencil sketch and then go over it in ink. I'll get them framed. Little simple black frames, I think."

"Uh . . . I don't know."

We were in the kitchen and she had turned to get something out of a cabinet. It must not have been there. *Slam.* I started toward my room. *Slam. SLAM.* Sixteen slams. We had loads of cabinets in our all-white kitchen, spacious cabinets with shiny chromium knobs. It was one of the things she had loved most about the house.

That night there was a light tap on my door, then Annie peered in.

"Come on in. What's up?"

She sat side-saddle on the end of my bed and looked at my wall. "Please do those pictures." Her voice sounded tired.

"Why? Why should I? She never does anything for me."

Annie examined her nails, then the inside of her palm.

"I'm sick of her," I said.

"I don't want her to go back to that place."

"So what if she goes back?"

Annie's shoulders slumped. I thought about patting her back, but my stomach knotted. "Why don't *you* make something for the bazaar?"

No answer.

"How 'bout some of those cute little bar pins like you made at

Girl Scouts? The ones with the person's name spelled in rice."

Nothing.

"Or maybe one of those acorn necklaces. Huh?"

"Grownups don't want things like that." She got up to leave.

"Annie?"

When she looked at me, there were two ruler-straight tear trails on her cheeks.

I crumbled. "Okay, okay, for god's sake. I'll do the drawings."

"Could you drive me over to Alder Drive this afternoon, Mother? I want to sketch that old brown cottage behind Mrs. Hoover's house."

"Honey, I can't. Etha Mae's leaving early to go to the dentist and people are coming to deliver donations."

"Maybe David can take me."

"Yes."

I was floored.

David chauffeured me, and when he saw my first picture, he was surprised. "You're good."

"Should I sign 'em Sarah Stein?"

"Sarah, come on."

I poked my nose against his cheek. "Only kidding."

"No you're not."

"Well, I don't understand why you won't tell your parents. My mother knows you're Jewish and the sky hasn't dropped."

"Does she care?"

"Oh, yeah. She says she doesn't want a passel of grandchildren running around in those little black beanies."

"Yarmulkes."

"Yarmulkes. Anyway, I told her not to worry, we aren't getting married."

I did two or three sketches of the cottage and then had him take me to the rock quarry. We hauled a blanket and my sketchbook down to the place we always went. I wanted to draw the cliff on the opposite side of the quarry and then go home and copy my cottage on top of it so it would look like a little English house on the white cliffs of Dover.

David was reading *The Scarlet Letter* for school, and when I put down my sketch pad, he closed his book and kissed me.

"Are we fighting today?" I asked.

"Nope."

He was wrong. It was our usual scene, the one we knew every line for after so many dress rehearsals. Trouble is, he wasn't acting but I was. I liked him touching me and it scared me. It felt so good that I let him unhook my bra and touch my skin. I let it go on about five minutes until I was dizzy and he was huffing, but I refused to let myself even breathe hard. I knew if I did, he'd know I liked it and push harder for me to go further. I had to pretend it was just OK, I could take it or leave. As soon as I stopped him, he started his whining. "Why not, Sarah? Please?"

I scrambled to my feet, adjusted my blouse and skirt, and gathered my pencils and pad. "I don't feel like doing this today."

Annie agreed to be a model for one of my pictures. I had sketched my chinaberry tree from memory, but it looked dull with the bat family hanging on that forlorn branch. It needed something else, a person. Annie found a low branch in our yard to perch on. "I feel silly," she said.

"I'm sure I would too, but try to make believe you're Rima the bird girl. Look dreamy or sleepy. Good. Now gaze up at the sky."

While I sketched away, it hit me that my little sister had gotten pretty. She was definitely thinner and her chestnut hair had grown shoulder-length. It framed her face and made her brown eyes stand out, soft and doe-like. "Wait'll you see this."

"That's not me!" she humphed.

"Oh yes it is; it's exactly you."

She looked pleased, but drew back into her shell fast. "My foot looks funny," she said, crabby. It did look more like a hoof than a human foot.

"I'll draw a branch in front of it."

I ended up with three pictures for Mother to put in the bazaar. The cottage on the cliff, Rima in the chinaberry, and a scene from my imagination: a shack in the flat Mississippi Delta with an old wringer washing machine on the porch, a scrawny chicken scratching in the yard.

Daddy brought me a soft gum eraser from his office to erase my pencil lines after I'd inked over them in black. "Those are wonderful, honey," he said, smiling.

Mother looked as though she wanted to hug me, but she stopped herself. The last time she had hugged me was after I almost drowned at Lake Rabun. I was five. "I'm proud of you," she said. "I really am."

The church bazaar was a success and all my pen-and-inks sold. Then Mother's upbeat period ended. Some afternoons I could hear her ice cubes rattling in her Tupperware glass. She was drinking again.

My father was insane. He wanted to have his company's Christmas party at our house. How could he imagine Mother planning and hosting a party when she was bombed by dinner every night? Once a week, he had to carry a bag with seven empty scotch bottles out to the garbage can. It was funny how she hid her cocktails in opaque glasses, yet made no effort to hide the polished off bottles. She just lined them up like bowling pins on the pantry floor.

"Chris and me can decorate the tree," Annie said.

"Chris and *I*," Mother corrected. "Robert Grimes is handling everything, sweetie pie. The tree, the flowers, the hors d'oeuvres. We can sit back and relax. He did an elegant tree at Fulton Bank last year."

Robert Grimes, a quiet little man, got no say. He and his assistants ran around like wind-up toys, dragging boxes from the attic, dashing out to Hinkle's for more garland, rewriting the food list a hundred times—all under Mother's command.

Robert suggested flocking the tree, Amelia, can you imagine?

She was back in touch with Amelia Martin, calling her and chatting like old times. She needed a friend to come to the glorious Christmas affair because she disliked Daddy's office people.

"You and your sister need new dresses," Mother announced.

"Do I *have* to come to the party?"

She glared. "We'll go to Rich's."

"Can I invite David?"

She was sitting in her favorite armchair in the den, sipping from a dark amber-colored glass. "Would it be OK to ask David?" she mocked. I walked out, but she continued. "Oh, yes, of course. Let's ask Sol too. And . . . hmmm . . . Al Moscowitz, the butcher. Yes, and the rabbi!" She cackled at the top of her lungs. "Come one, come all, we're celebrating Baby Jesus!"

I about-faced and stomped back to the den. "You're no better than the Blumes. You're every bit as prejudiced. You hate Jews as much as they hate us."

She stared at me, bewildered, her whiskey-soaked brain obviously reeling at the idea that *they* might actually dislike *us*. I fled, expecting her to recover and come after me, but she didn't. I never mentioned the party to David.

"Sarah, please circulate; you are a hostess too, remember. Etha Mae, could you please empty ashtrays again? And would you . . . Mae!"

"Yessum?"

"Where is the garnish? That platter looks naked."

Etha Mae dutifully fetched parsley from the kitchen as Mother clomped off in her new shoes. "She's been after you, after you, Mae. All week! You shouldn't put up with her talking to you like that. Why don't you stand up to her?"

She shook her head. "Yo mama's still grievin' 'bout Miz Teal, honey. I jus' pray for her."

Chris sauntered in looking like the boss's son in his school blazer and club tie. "You got any chips, Mae?"

Etha Mae ruffled his curls. "Lawd, Mister Chris, yo mama would kill me if I was to bring out chips after Mister Robert brought all this fancy food."

Thank god, for my father's sake, everything went smoothly, especially when you consider that my mother hated company; company messed things up. But that night the architects and their wives had the good manners not to put wet glasses on her mahogany tables or let their ashes flutter to the floor.

Mother's friend Amelia introduced me to her husband as "a

budding artist." She told him I was planning to study art. My only response was to stammer.

"Now don't forget we have the Art Institute right here."

"I haven't really thought about college yet, Mrs. Martin."

"We were thrilled with your pen-and-inks. They were in the silent auction, you know."

I had no idea what a silent auction was, but I knew where Mrs. Martin had gotten the art school idea. Apparently, Mother was now telling people I was going to be the next "great American artist." Was she moving me into Ben's place? I wasn't sure I wanted to be there.

Part Five

And now a bubble burst,
and now the world.

Alexander Pope, *Essay on Man*

CHAPTER 20

*A*nn Odom called the morning after my parents' party, which had gone surprisingly well. "They're back and they know everything," she said.

"Who's back?" I whispered; Mother lurked nearby whenever a call was for me.

"My parents, dumb-dumb. They know loads of kids were here. They know about the liquor."

"How'd they find out?"

"Look, it's a long story. I'll give you the lowdown at school. They got suspicious when my mother found Bobby's socks under their bed."

"Couldn't they have been your father's?"

"He doesn't wear that kind."

"Oh my god. Are you grounded forever?"

"Not really."

"You slay me! I can't wait to hear how you wriggled out of this. Want to do something on New Year's Eve?"

"I can't."

"I thought you weren't grounded."

"Um, Sarah . . ."

"Yeah?"

"They won't let me hang around with you anymore."

"Me?"

"'Cause you were my spend-the-night company, they think you

cooked up the party. 'The instigator,' my father said."

"Did you tell him I wasn't?"

"Sarah, all my life, whenever I've gotten caught doing something, my parents blamed somebody else. You're the unlucky one this time."

"That's not fair! I'm the only one who wasn't getting drunk and puking all night! Or screwing!!"

"Cool it, Sar. This'll blow over. It always does."

I wanted to break something. Instead I went to the den and slipped one of Mother's cigarettes out of her pack. I could hear her opening an ice tray in the kitchen. Back in my room I lit up and stood by the window so the smoke would go out, my hand shaking. I couldn't understand Ann's parents. Dr. Odom had never been friendly to me, but he was rude to everybody. Her mother had been nice enough, though, and I couldn't believe she'd want to pin this on me. I scraped the cigarette out on my window screen, flushed the butt down the toilet, and called Ann back.

"I want to talk to your mother. Can you get her?"

"Why?"

"I'm really upset about this. It's not fair, and I know she likes me. She'll listen. She'll believe me when I tell her this wasn't my fault. Look, I'll tell the truth. It's the best thing to do in a case like this. I'll say you invited a few people to drop by and, boom, a whole bunch showed up."

"That's not such a great idea. I think we should drop it, let it blow over. Really. Sar, I gotta go."

"Mother, David wants me to go to a movie Friday."

"That's Christmas Eve," she snapped. "Does he know that?"

"Yes."

"I think you should be with your family. Tell David that Christmas Eve is a family time."

"I'm going."

"I beg your pardon?"

"Everybody has dates. I'm sick of being the only one who doesn't."

"Don't push me."

"You wouldn't let me cross the street till I was ten. I'm not waiting till I'm twenty-five to date!"

I slammed the double doors to the den. She never said a word about it, and by Friday afternoon I was petrified, worrying about how she'd act when David came to the door. Around five, I walked past the den, and there she sat, sipping from her favorite glass. She didn't look at me, but I know she saw me. "*Oy, oy*, Blumenfeld," she chanted. "*Oy, oy, mazle tov*."

I walked to the den door. She pretended I wasn't there, stood up, and closed the door in my face. Then she burst into loud, operatic song. "*Oy, oy*, Blumenschtein; *oy, oy, mazle tov*."

I crept back to the living room to wait for David, my heart hammering. "Blumenfeld" and "Blumenschtein" were obviously twisted versions of Blume, David's last name. The other words sounded German. When the doorbell rang, I hurried to the front door to get out of there fast.

"Hey, David." I stumbled out, almost knocked him over.

"What's wrong, Sarah?"

"Let's get out of here."

With that, the door swung open.

"Hello, David."

"Hi, Mrs. Claiborne."

"You kids have a good time!"

"Thank you," he said politely.

I held my breath and kept walking.

"Merry Christmas!" she sang out, emphasizing the word "Christmas."

"Same to you," he said.

He asked why I was jumpy. "I was just ready to get out of there, you know?"

We weren't really going to the movies. David had checked the paper to see what was at the Piedmont Drive-In, in case my mother asked. It was a movie he'd seen, *Spartacus*. "It's about slaves rebelling in the Roman Empire."

"What else?"

"Let's see. It was in the days of gladiators. Kirk Douglas is in it; I don't remember who else. Tony Curtis, maybe. Tell her the chariot races were exciting but you hated the blood."

We drove downtown to see the tree on top of Rich's and the Christmas lights in the stores. David had borrowed his father's Oldsmobile. "Slide over," he said, patting the seat beside him. I moved close to him and he rested his hand on my knee. "Let's start here at Five Points and drive all the way out Peachtree to Brookhaven."

"That's fine, I don't care."

"Sarah, you need to get over this Ann thing."

"I can't. It's not fair. Now I have zero friends and I'll be trapped at home."

"You've got me."

"Yeah, to sneak around with."

"I'm going to tell my parents."

I looked at him. "When?"

"Real soon."

At Oglethorpe, the Gothic-looking college in Brookhaven, David turned off Peachtree and drove a few blocks into a residential neighborhood. "I've got a surprise for you."

I felt empty and too numb to ask where we were going. He could drive me to New York; Chicago; Okeechobee, Florida. It didn't matter. Suddenly the pavement turned to gravel and narrowed. We bounced along, winding through woods. At the end of the road there was a clearing and our headlights beamed out over a body of water. David cut the engine and we were left in yellow, neon-sign moonlight. "Let's walk down to the lake," he said, getting out and offering me his hand. I took it and slid out under the steering wheel.

The shimmering water with the moon on it looked like liquid silver. "This is unreal," I whispered. I thought we might be trespassing.

"Like it?"

"Yes."

When he kissed me, I didn't kiss back. It was cold out, but I felt as limp as you'd feel on a broiling day in July. Back in the car we listened to the radio; I rested my head on his shoulder. After a while he reached into the back seat and retrieved a box wrapped in Christmas paper. It was a beautiful, soft Angora sweater—cream-colored. I pressed it to my cheek. "I love it, David! But I'm embarrassed. I left yours at home." I had nothing for him. I didn't think we'd be exchanging gifts.

"I love you," he said, and we made out a little. I felt obligated.

On Christmas morning I stayed in bed. Why get up? There were no friends to get together with, and I dreaded the scene when we got to

Ben's gifts—three small, flat packages for Chris, Annie, and me wrapped in holly berry tissue paper. Plus, I had cramps and a headache. I limped to my bathroom, took three aspirin, and got back in bed.

Chris came to wake me first, his corkscrew curls vibrating atop his wired up little body.

"I'm sick," I told him.

Annie tried next. "I'm not celebrating Christmas this year," I told her. Then Daddy came in but left fast, blushing when I complained about "girl troubles." Mother, unlike the others, didn't inquire after my health. She marched in and yanked up the Venetian blinds. *Thrupppp.*

"Rise and shine!"

I covered my face with my forearm. "I'm nauseous. I'd better stay put."

She tee-heed and pinched my toe through the covers. "Too much partying last night?"

I held my breath.

"We're bringing the gifts back here."

"*No*, Mother, I'm sick."

"All right, only one then. Edward!"

She paraded down the hall and was back in two minutes with a large dress box wrapped in gold foil and red velvet ribbon. "This is my gift to the whole family." She thrust it at me.

"Annie, you do it," I said. "I'm woozy."

Mother didn't protest, so Annie sat beside me on the edge of the bed. When she pulled out my "Girl in Chinaberry Tree" drawing, I gulped. Matted and framed it seemed much bigger.

"Oh, Catherine, that's grand," Daddy said.

"I thought this sold in the auction," I said, not looking at her.

"It did; to me. I wasn't about to let it go, so I bid high."

"How much?"

"Never mind. It's a gift."

"Can I go back to my stuff?" Chris whined.

"Go ahead. Well, what do you think?"

"I'm surprised," I said.

"I'm just tickled to death to have it," Mother said.

Later, she sent Daddy in with a tray for me. Scrambled eggs, apple juice, a hot cross bun.

"I can't eat all this."

"Try eating a little something, honey," he said.

"Daddy? Would you bring me my package from Ben?"

It was a nice paperback copy of *The Stranger* like the one he had in New Orleans. I put it on the bedside table. When Mother came in, she picked it up and skimmed the back cover as though she were mildly interested.

"Sarah, your doing artwork for the bazaar meant so much to me. You just don't know. I was so proud to be able to brag on my child."

I flipped over, my back to her.

"No one . . . no one, unless they've experienced it, could comprehend—"

"Mother!"

"To be shut out by a child, one you've been so close to . . . I had such high hopes for your brother."

"Could we not talk about Ben?"

"It's so horribly painful every day. But on Christmas! And then he sends books to you three and not one thing for your father! Forget *me*."

"Mother, please, I'm sick."

"You are cold. You've gotten so cold. And hard. Just you wait.

When you have children and one pulls something like this on you . . ." She hovered over me. I dragged myself up and went toward my bathroom.

"I don't plan to tell my children they're adopted," I said over my shoulder. I slammed myself in the bathroom, turned on the faucet, and let the water run. She came to the door and talked through it.

"What did you say?"

I turned off the water. "You heard me."

Then there was silence, and I waited a long time to come out.

"Sit down on this bed and repeat what you said."

"You told him he was adopted. He left because . . . it's *all your fault.*" I shrieked so loud it forced a gush of menstrual blood out of me. I dashed back into the bathroom to see if I'd ruined my underpants and gown.

Instead of bangs and crashes in my bedroom, I heard Mother laughing, high-pitched like a hyena. I came back out. "He believed that?" she asked, not waiting for the answer. She hee-hawed and slapped her thigh, bent over and held her stomach. The saying, "laughed so hard I bust a gut" occurred to me.

"It's *not* funny."

"Are you telling me Ben believed that story?"

"For god's sake, you showed him the papers."

She shut up. You could see her thinking, casting her mind back to that day. "Your brother isn't adopted. Would you care to see his birth certificate?"

"Why'd you let him go on believing it?"

"I had no idea he would believe that. It was a joke! I dragged out some papers. I don't know . . . something on official-looking stationery. About PTA, maybe. I was bluffing. It was a joke. I never dreamed—"

"A joke? A *joke*? It wrecked our family."

She ignored me. "Daughter dear, you have made my day! This is so easily repaired. Your father will contact Ben and straighten this out."

"Daddy, how can you call Ben? He doesn't have a phone."

He was concentrating on gluing a piece of wood trim on an end table that Chris had accidentally broken off. "Sweetie, I have to wait until he's back at work."

"Didn't you tell him he wasn't adopted? Back when I told you?"

"Yes, but he didn't say much."

"Uh . . . Daddy? Would you do me a favor? Don't tell him how Mother heard about this, OK?"

"I don't think he'd ask about that, honey?"

"If he asks, tell him Mother just mentioned out of the blue that she hoped he didn't believe her joke."

"I don't want to lie, Sarah."

"Daddy! He's going to hate me."

"I don't think so, honey."

I stormed out of his workshop and pounded up the basement steps. He lived in a little world where everything had to line up on the page—the perfect slots where the cars went, the straight halls that people walked down. I'd like to live in his crisp blueprint world. Maybe in that place aunts and uncles love you, grandmothers are sweet, mothers pal around with you. What if I were perfect like Daddy, didn't want to lie? Well, for one thing, I'd sit down and write Ben the truth: "I can't read that book you sent because it reminds me of my miserable trip to see you." I would also tell Mother I had no desire to be an artist. I'd inform Ann Odom that I hated her parents' guts.

That night, Christmas night, I didn't sleep. I turned and flipped and threw off covers, got cold, pulled them back up, turned again, plumped my pillow, smushed it back down. My gown twisted around me. A pathetic little Shirley Temple voice kept saying in my ear, "Ben might come back." My own normal voice answered it, "Shut up, you idiot!"

In the morning I went to the kitchen to get some juice and toast. Mother accosted me. "Sarah! Sarah, stand right there. When I get Ben on the line, I'm turning the phone over to you."

"I don't want to talk."

"Tell your brother this adoption business is preposterous."

"You tell him."

"He'll hang up."

"He has no phone."

"I can reach him. I have an emergency number."

"No, I'm not talking to him."

I went to my room; I wanted to eat and go back to bed. My cramps were bad and aspirin did nothing. Sleep was the only cure. When Mother burst in, I jumped and sloshed orange juice on my bedspread. "Put that down. Get up." She ripped off the covers—the spread, the blanket, the top sheet—and grabbed at me. "Get up!" She hauled me by my forearm across the room toward the phone. With my other hand, I caught her free wrist and clamped my fingers around it. She had a piece of paper with the phone number on it in that hand.

"Drop it," I yelled.

"Let me go. You're talking to your brother today if I have to tie you down. EDWARD!"

Daddy came in wiping his hands on a dish towel. Mother and I were locked together, circling like wrestlers.

"Help me here for god's sake, Edward."

"Catherine . . ."

"Drop the friggin' paper, Mother."

She let go of my arm and tried to slap me across the face, but I drew back and the blow connected with my ear. I dropped to my knees, holding my ear. She bopped me again on top of my head. That brought Daddy into the fray, finally; he grabbed her wrists. "Catherine, Catherine," he said softly as if to soothe her. She was like a bull. She tore free of his hold and slapped at him, missing his cheek and sending his glasses flying across the room.

"No," she bellowed. "No! No! No!" Out she charged, down the hall and into the bathroom. I took off after her and pounded on the door with both fists.

"Come out of there. Come out now. You made this mess. You caused this," I screamed into the crack between the door and the jamb. "You caused this goddam trouble."

"Sarah, go on back to your room, honey." Daddy was behind me, patting my shoulder. My ear throbbed. I turned and pushed past him. I surveyed the mess in my room, and started to cry. Since I hurt too bad to re-make the bed, I dropped down on the mound of covers on the floor.

When I woke up, it was dark and the house was quiet. I went to the kitchen and made a toasted cheese sandwich because there was no sign of dinner, no sign of anyone. Annie was probably at Dee's, but I wondered where Daddy and Chris were. Mother was likely in her bed, lying in the dark with a damp cloth over her eyes. I ate fast standing at the counter, then went back to my room. I wanted to shower, but I thought Mother might creep in and stab me through the curtain.

CHAPTER 21

*T*he next morning I called David. His mother answered. "Who's calling?"

"Sarah Stein."

"One moment."

"Hello?"

"David, can you come get me?"

"Now?"

"Yes. I'm walking down to Estes School. Pick me up there in thirty minutes."

"Are you OK?"

"See ya in a half hour."

David was late so I paced around the school building three times—fast, to stay warm. Everyone who drove by stared, carloads of cheerful families headed for department stores to exchange Christmas gifts. Finally, David pulled up.

"I look awful. Didn't roll my hair last night."

"What's going on?"

"Big fight."

"About?"

"About nothing. My mother's nuts."

"What's in the bag?"

"A bottle of her scotch."

"God, Sarah."

"Hey, stop at the Dairy Queen, would you?"

"Are you trying to get grounded? Then I'll never see you."

"I won't get grounded." I had David get me a chili dog and a giant cup of ice. "Let's go out to that lake again."

"What's going on? Was the fight about us?"

"No. I just had to get out. Can you crank up the heat?"

"We won't be able to stay long; it's freezing."

The lake looked bleak in the daylight. "Keep the car running."

"We can't sit in here with the windows shut."

"Then drive. Get out there and just drive, 'cause I plan to finish this bottle."

David took off his gloves and put his hand on my cheek. I turned toward him and he put his other hand on my face. He held me like that, stared into my eyes, and kissed me as though he hoped his lips would work magic and I'd straighten up. "What are you trying to prove?"

"Could you close your window?"

After a half hour he insisted we go. I had him drive out to the fringes of north Atlanta, past warehouses and truck stops, then trailer parks and shacks.

"Oh, look, let's go there! Maybe Pauline the Palm Reader can tell me my future."

"Sarah, you're going to be sick. Let me . . . how much of that have you had?"

I couldn't answer because I didn't know, and I couldn't hold up the bottle because my hands were little rubber duckies hanging off my wrists. "Quack."

"What?"

"Wack, wack."

"I'm taking you home."

When I opened my eyes, we were parked a few blocks from my house. "Home again, home again, jiggity, jig . . ."

"Sarah, I'm going up your driveway and stopping at the back door. You need to get out and walk inside."

"Home again, home again."

"If your mother sees my car, I'm dead, but I can't leave you on the street. I don't trust you to go home."

Just then my chili dog started up. I was able to get the door open, but that was it. David scrambled around to my side and opened the door all the way. "Oh, god." He put his hand on my shoulder but stepped back as I heaved.

"I'm sorry. I'm sorry," I said, sobbing and choking. But throwing up was good; it helped stop the spinning, and when David let me out I was able to walk from the back door to my bedroom. I got right into bed, clothes and all.

I don't know what time it was when the overhead light in my bedroom clicked on, I couldn't open my eyes due to the glowing coal chunks in the top of my head, which throbbed in time with my heartbeat. And my ear was killing me. A pocket knife seemed to be whittling inside my ear. My thoughts dropped to my mouth, the rancid chili taste and something else like burnt logs. I smacked my swollen lips and concentrated on my toes as a diversion to help me fall back into sleep. Good, black sleep.

"I've called Mrs. Blume."

Open. Open your eyes.

"I have informed her of your condition when her son dropped you off at the back door like a package."

I tried but my eyes wouldn't open.

"Get up now. Clean yourself up."

I woke up several times, briefly, conscious of my overhead light, wanting to get up and flip it off, but it seemed too far to go. Once, I got up to use the bathroom and managed to kick off my loafers, but I needed to get back under the covers. The house was cold so I left on my red wool jumper and knee socks.

"She stole our scotch! Thievin' little . . ." The shouting seemed to be in a dream, but then Mother was there yanking the covers back, whapping at my legs with a belt. The buckle hit my shin and I screamed and stood up in my bed.

"Whore. Drunken . . . lying . . . thieving whore!"

Daddy rushed in, then Annie.

"Stop, stop," Daddy pleaded. He reached for Mother but she whirled around and the belt lashed his side. He drew back with his arm up.

Annie was sobbing and jumping up and down in the doorway. "Stop it, Mama!" she wailed.

Mother turned her attention back to me. I had stumbled off the bed and scuttled across the room to the wall like a stupid rat cornering itself. She whipped the belt at my legs and I jumped from one foot to the other trying to dodge it. In the midst of her cursing me and Annie screaming, I thought about how I must look like Gabby Hayes in a bar scene, dancing a jig to hop over flying bullets. I laughed.

"You lying . . . *whap* . . . whoring . . . *whap* . . . gutter trash!"

I grabbed the belt. Now it was a tug of war.

"You're the trash," I bellowed. I wanted the belt, wanted to beat her to a pulp. Annie had shut up and was watching with her mouth agape. Daddy cowered in the corner repeating "Catherine, Catherine" like a stuck record.

"You lied to Ben. You ruined our family. YOU'RE THE NASTY, LYIN' BITCH."

She couldn't pull the belt away from me, so she started moving in on it, hand over hand, working toward me. She was an arm's length away when she dropped her end of the belt and began flailing her hands at my head. I charged around her, past Daddy, past Annie, down the hall and out the back door.

I couldn't get far in my socks, so I circled the block, turned up Dee's driveway, and through her yard. I tore through the woods into our backyard and into the storage shed behind our garage. The sun was just coming up and I prayed Dee's parents hadn't been sitting at their breakfast table watching. My parents were obviously not aware that Chris had turned the shed into a fort; several times over the next few hours I heard Daddy calling for me, and doors opening and closing in the garage.

Other than being cold, Chris's hideout was all right. He had Moon Pies and Cokes in it, a camp mattress, an army blanket. Everything I needed but something to read other than comic books. Also, some aspirin would have been nice. The bloody gashes up and down my legs were of no concern to me. When I looked down at them, they seemed to be someone else's.

I did have a plan. At some point they had to go out. Then I would slip in, shower, dress, and call Ben. I knew the name of the company where he worked, so I would get the number from the long distance operator. I would ask him to send money to Laurie's house. I could easily walk that far and stay with her till the money came. Then she and Roy could drive me to Brookwood Station; I would take the train to New Orleans. Ben would take me in and I would tell him about Russell so he'd never leave me alone with him. I could get a job, maybe as a waitress, or do pen-and-inks to sell in Pirate's Alley.

It was Chris who found me. "I knew you were here, Sally!"

"Ssshh."

"I knew it all the time. Didja eat the Moon Pies?"

"Yeah."

"That's OK. Did you run away?"

"What's going on in there, Chris?"

"Huh? Umm . . . Daddy took the door off."

"What door?"

"The bathroom. I watched him. It was neat. Ya know those big nail things in—"

"Why'd he take it off?"

"Mama fell asleep in the tub. The police are after you, Sally."

"What?"

"Daddy called 'em."

"Chris, can you go in there and pretend you never saw me?"

"Sure."

"Go in there and get Annie to sneak out here, would you?"

"She's over at Dee's."

"Oh, god. Chris, go see if you can smuggle out a banana or something."

My next visitor was my father. "Sarah, please come inside."

"No."

"Honey, the police are combing Atlanta for you. I need to call them. Please, come in."

"Is she in there? I'm not coming in. Look at my legs. LOOK, Daddy!"

"She's quieted down."

"Quieted down? If I come in she'll kill me." I was shuddering. I burped Moon Pie and thought I might throw up so I cupped my hands over my mouth. Daddy just stood there. He looked like he hadn't slept in days. His face was gray and he had whiskers. I'd never seen him with any beard. It was stubbly and white. He stood there looking like a lost hobo, then left. Minutes later he was back to tell me that Mother was asleep; he said I could go to my room and she wouldn't bother me.

After I bandaged my legs I packed an overnight bag and convinced Daddy to drive me to Laurie's house. He wanted to know if they were expecting me, which they weren't, but I lied and said yes. Ann Odom taught me well.

Of course they let me spend the night—quite a few, in fact—especially after they saw my legs. I showed Laurie and her mother so they could be witnesses if I decided to sue Mother for beating me. Even in her drunken haze, Laurie's mom was shocked and said I could stay as long as I wanted to.

I called Daddy at his office on Monday and asked him to bring me more clothes. He said he would and I gave him a list. Not more than an hour later he called back and said Mother had made an appointment for me with a shrink, some doctor who specialized in helping "troubled teens," he said.

"I'm not troubled, Daddy! Mother's the one who needs help, for god's sake, not me! I'm *not* going!" I yelled, and slammed the phone down.

Dr. Verner's office was downtown. I had to ride the bus from Laurie's neighborhood, then walk two blocks to get there. Dr. Verner was business-like, which was fine. She had a thick German accent. I don't know how long she'd been in Atlanta, but after fifteen minutes I realized she didn't know she was living in the land of phonies. Step right up for your Coca-Cola and your Southern fried lies. If she'd just started working on people's brains in this town, she was in for a surprise. They'll tell her, "Everything's wonderful, everything's fine," when it's not. I'm sure Mother's country club pals have gruesome secrets they cover up too.

"What do you want to do, Sarah?" She said "what" and "want" like they started with a "v."

"I want to stay at Laurie's."

"That's your friend."

"Un-huh."

"Have her parents agreed to let you live there?"

"Uh . . ."

"What would have to happen for you to go home?"

"Mother would move out."

"You don't feel you can be there with her."

"No." Mother found Dr. Verner. I knew Mother's tricks, so I was sure she had convinced her that *she* was normal and I was the nut case. "I'm worried about Annie and Chris too."

"Why is that, Sarah?"

"She's insane. She's going to kill someone, maybe even my father. Why won't anyone believe me? Look!" I pulled up my skirt to show her the belt marks. "This is nothing! My legs were solid black the day after she beat me. And these lines—see these lines? These were all bloody, sliced open.

"I don't know what Mother told you about all this, Dr. Verner;

maybe she said I was in a wreck or something. But there's something you need to know: everything that comes out of her mouth is a lie. If lies were fire our house would've burned to the ground by now."

Her mouth twitched. Maybe she thought I was exaggerating.

"I'm serious. You can't believe her. She probably charmed you; she fools people."

"And what about you, Sarah? Do you lie?"

I caught my breath, felt my face turning red. "Uh . . . yeah."

She raised her eyebrows.

"Mostly to my mother," I said. "I have to. My friend Ann taught me that."

After two appointments with me, Dr. Verner talked to Daddy. Then she saw me and Daddy together. Daddy made out like it wasn't so bad. Mother had been through a lot, he told her. Cancer, burying a dear friend.

"How about when she choked me, Daddy? Huh? What about that? I couldn't swallow for a week!"

He hung his head.

"And Ben. How 'bout that big lie to Ben, running him off?"

He looked at Dr. Verner. "My son." As if to remind her who Ben was.

"Mr. Claiborne, Sarah says she has been unhappy for a long time."

He glanced at me, sheepish, didn't say a word. He picked at a cuticle and stared out the window. Dr. Verner's office looked out on the famous Fox Theatre. What was he thinking? Was he wondering about the turrets, how they were constructed?

"Do you think your wife has been inordinately strict with Sarah?"

He looked at her and sighed. "I don't know. I've been away from home a good bit, traveling . . . for my work. I guess I . . . I didn't know Catherine and Sarah were fighting."

He turned to me looking so sad I wanted to cry, but I just gritted my teeth. On the way home he chatted about nothing, asked if I wanted to stop for a butter pecan cone when we passed Liggett's Drugs. I was numb. How could he act like this was a fun outing?

"Mother needs to go back to Breen and stay there till she's fixed," I said.

"She won't go, honey. I've tried."

"You asked her?"

"Yes. I *have* tried, Sarah."

"She's got to get help, Daddy; she has to! Did you tell Dr. Verner about her locking herself in the bathroom? After she sent me out to the waiting room, did you tell her about that?"

"No."

"Did y'all talk about *me*? Does she think *I'm* crazy?"

"She thinks you're very upset."

The day I finally moved home, Mother treated me like a patient who'd been hospitalized and returned after a long illness. "Don't worry with those things, dear, I'll have Etha Mae unpack for you later. Don't you want to crawl into bed?"

"No."

"Why don't you lie down and rest and I'll bring your dinner in later?"

"I'm not tired."

She shrugged and closed the door—gently. I thought about calling David. I'd been afraid to call him from Laurie's, afraid his mother would answer. I doubt that he'd tried to call here. Instead, I went to Annie's room. "Hey, can I come in?" She didn't look at me. "Whatcha readin'?" She held up the book—*Black Beauty*. "I loved that. Are you mad at me?" No answer. "Glad I'm home?"

"No."

"Why not, Annie? Mother beats me and you're angry at me?"

"I wish you were still at Laurie's."

"So do I!"

She stared at me with hard eyes. "It's peaceful around here when you're gone."

"I'll bet it is." I wanted to slam her door, but I just grinned and told her to go to hell as I ambled out. Next I headed for the basement.

"Lawd have mercy, Miss Sarah." Etha Mae ran around the ironing board to hug me and I clung to her waist. She smelled of starch. "What's wrong, chil'? Why you cryin'?"

"I missed you."

"Honey, what in the world?"

I wiped my eyes with the back of my hand and went to my stool. I didn't know how much she'd been told, but I wanted to tell everything. I thought how nice it would be to shrink into an infant and rest in her wide lap, listen to her singing. She waddled into her bathroom and came out with a wad of toilet paper. "I need some tissues. I . . ." I tooted my nose hard, which drowned out her words, and we laughed.

"That boy gone and broke your heart. I know, Miss Sarah."

"Who?"

"Mister David."

"No! Did Mother say that?"

"Chil', she told me."

231

"Etha Mae, Mother and I had a bad fight and I ran away."

She put the iron down. "Miss Sarah?"

She looked like a child, let down on Christmas morning. Telling her Mother beat me—and hit Daddy—would wreck her. "My best friend, Ann, got in trouble and she's not allowed to do anything with me. I hate my school. I yelled at Mother and she popped me."

"Chil', sometimes I fuss my head off with Pack when he didn't do a thing. Maybe my feet hurt. Maybe I missed the No.10. Not a thing to do with him. Yo mama knows you love her. Now don't you feel bad 'cause you all fussed. I put you on the prayer chain last week. We all praying for you at my church. Lord Jesus is watching over you—right now, right while we're sittin' here."

It was the first time I'd ever spent time with Mae that Mother didn't call me to come upstairs; maybe it was because she was busy cooking my favorite dinner—Southern fried chicken, rice and gravy, fresh green beans.

That night, everyone at the table was quiet but her. "I can't decide where to hang Sarah's 'Chinaberry Girl.' What do you think, Ed?"

"The living room? Over the piano?"

"That's a thought. I considered the study, between the two windows. Maybe the front hall . . ."

Annie and I hurried to clear the dishes afterwards and scattered to our rooms, leaving Daddy with the kitchen. Mother had already gone to her chair in the den, where she still posted herself every night until everyone else was in bed. She broke her habit and knocked on my door about ten o'clock. She had my grandmother's jewelry box, the one that looked like a treasure chest. I had loved it and asked to have it a few times, but Mother said it was very old and "too precious for a child." It was dark wood with tiny inlaid mother-of-pearl flowers along the top and sides.

"Your father's mother got this in Europe when she turned twenty and took the Grand Tour with her aunt. She gave it to me when Edward and I married; I think she wishes she had it back!"

"Why?"

"Oh, I think she felt generous at that moment. But parting with something dear would not be typical of her, as you know." She set the box on my bed and then carefully turned it over. "Did you know it has a music box? Listen." She twisted a silver key, turned the box back over, and opened the top. Some minuet-ish tune started to play. "I want you to have this."

"Why?" I asked, blasé.

"As a thank-you for doing the drawings."

I cranked the music key and it began playing another unknown melody. "Thanks, thanks a lot." If I told her I'd always wanted it, she'd probably cackle and walk out saying "Only kidding, you can't have it."

That night I dreamed I owned a horse, a beautiful roan. I loved him so much I could feel my love pouring out on him as I rode him bareback. We galloped off—too fast—so I hung onto his mane. "Whoa, boy," I said, but he kept on. I clung to his neck screaming stop, and finally he did, but then he jerked his head down to pitch me off. When I fell, he started pawing and kicking at me, so I ran into a barn and up into a loft. He chased me in and reared up on his hind legs trying to get at me. An old man was watching.

"Why does he hate me?" I yelled over the crashing hoofs and splintering wood.

The man smiled. "He doesn't hate you. He loves you."

The horse started crashing into the beams that held up the ledge I was perched on. I knew that if it collapsed the horse would stomp me to death. Maybe the only way to survive was to aim for his back, jump down and ride him, hang on and ride. He couldn't trample me if I was on his back. I realized I might have to ride him for the rest of my life. Never be able to get off. The loft began giving way, crumbling. I was falling fast, then woke up gasping.

On the day I was to start back to school, I decided to call Ben. Now I was sure that moving to New Orleans and starting a new life would be the best thing for me—in spite of the jewelry box peace-offering, in spite of Mother being nice when I said I didn't feel like going to school. From my bed, I could hear Etha Mae vacuuming the hall, and Mother interrupting her to say she was off to the bank and post office.

As soon as she left I got up and wandered through the house. It was strange being back in the Claiborne museum again after the weeks at Laurie's. Her mother had given up cleaning; she spent her days in front of TV soap operas, or flicking down cards in solitaire rows on the kitchen table. Towers of dishes teetered in the sink, and dust fuzzed up the tops of the furniture. I didn't care; at least the place wasn't a tomb.

When Mother got home after lunch, she popped her head in my room to check on me.

"I ate some gumbo. I feel OK now," I told her.

"Well, I don't. I may have caught your bug. I'm going to soak in a hot tub."

Mother always got sick soon after one of us did. Odd how that worked. Of course, nursing ailing children can be exhausting.

I placed the call to Ben's office from my room. The long distance operator found the number and soon I heard a woman saying, "LeFevre and Company." The second the operator told her it was a person-to-person call for Ben Claiborne, I panicked. How could I explain everything that had happened over the phone? The secretary put us on hold but came back on in a minute to say Mr. Claiborne wouldn't be in that day. Mr. Claiborne!

I had to talk to Ben. Now. I slipped into Mother and Daddy's room. The first thing my eyes fell on was the bedside table where she kept her address book and special newspaper clippings, like the one about her father when he died. It was brown with age, and its pinking-sheared edges had started falling off like rotten teeth. The emergency number would be in that drawer for sure, or stuck in her Bible. There was no sound coming from the bathroom, so I assumed she was lolling in the tub.

As I bent over to look in the drawer, the door from the bathroom opened, and there stood Mother wearing nothing but her housecoat—not buttoned. I walked out of the slot between the twin beds, my eyes glued on her chest where her breast used to be. It was like a ditch, all scooped out. Down in it were dark purple scars. It looked like someone hacked her breast off with a hatchet. Instead of covering herself, she whipped the robe open and stalked toward me. "Get a good look at it, why don't you? Get a good, long look at it!"

I tore out of the room, back into my own. I knew she would come after me, so I went to my back window and opened it. Maybe I could make it to Dee's, hide in her garage until she got home from school, have her call Annie to bring me some clothes. I unlatched the screen and shoved, but it didn't budge. I pushed again. Nothing. I noticed a shiny dot in the corner of the screen frame. A nail head glinting in the sun. Two inches above that, another nail head. Another and another. I closed the window hard; then came the knock on my door.

"Sarah, what was that crash? Let me in."

"NO!"

"What were you doing in my room?"

I didn't answer.

"I believe you owe me an explanation."

I walked over to the door and shouted through it. "I'm sorry! I thought you were in the tub!"

"That's not what I asked you."

I couldn't think of one good reason to have been in her room. "I wanted the number, OK?"

"What number?"

"Ben's."

"Open the door." She sounded almost bored. "I don't have the number."

"Liar!"

"For your information, I destroyed it. Ben's not interested in being a member of this family. 'Well, fine,' I say, because I'm no longer interested in being his mother. As far as I'm concerned your brother is dead. Dead and buried!"

Mother left a dinner tray outside my door that night, like June Cleaver would do if Beaver were in a snit. She even spoke in June's voice through the crack. "You're being childish, Sarah. Now eat this good meal and get to bed. The carpool comes early."

That night I lay in bed wide awake thinking about what I'd seen. I hadn't thought about how it would look to have one breast. Well, maybe I had. Maybe I'd imagined a flat, blank spot. Or one clean, straight line. Sometimes when I looked in the mirror I thought bosoms looked like two big eyes. Maybe I had thought Mother's would be like one eye open and one eye shut, like a wink. What did *she* think when she looked in the mirror? Did she avoid looking? I fought off sleep, afraid I would dream about her carved out chest . . . or the roan horse.

Annie shook me out of a half-sleep. "There's a funny smell in the house."

It was black in my room and in the hall behind her. I blinked until I focused on her outline beside my bed. "You're waking me up to tell me—"

"It smells like smoke."

I flared my nostrils and sniffed hard. "I don't smell a thing." I could hear Daddy snoring through the wall. He snored like a cartoon character, like rumbling thunder. My glow-in-the-dark clock said two o'clock. "Sleep, Annie."

"Sarah!"

"Good grief." I dragged out of bed and down the hall behind Annie, aiming for the crack of light under her door. I didn't dare turn on the hall light and risk rousing Mother. When Annie opened her door, it did smell funny. I opened her other door, the one to the back hall, and closed it again fast—the hall was solid smoke. "Oh, god. DADDY!"

I towed Annie down the hall by the wrist and barged into my parents' room. Mother wasn't in her bed. Daddy instructed us to get Chris and go outside, out the front door; his voice was shaky.

Two fire trucks arrived, including a hook and ladder, and an ambulance. We three kids sat on the frost-covered lawn in our pajamas, huddled under the blanket I'd snatched off Chris's bed. We had giant oak trees around our house, and I noticed how small Chris and Annie and I seemed in comparison.

The firemen wouldn't let us go back in the house, and Mother needed to go right to the hospital. She was alive but they were concerned about her lungs. In the confusion of who would ride with Mother and where we could go, Mr. Teal came across the street and spoke to Daddy. We ended up spending the rest of the night in his den, sipping hot chocolate, watching Chris sleep on the couch, and listening for the phone.

One fire truck was still in our turnaround when Mae walked up the driveway. She was upset and cried but Daddy assured her Mother was going to be OK. They wanted to keep her in the hospital for a few days.

The fire marshal thought she'd fallen asleep and dropped a live cigarette. What was left of her favorite chair was still smoldering on the patio. The firemen had opened every window in the house and turned on the attic fan. By morning they'd said we could safely go back in.

Annie was sitting at the breakfast room table staring into her bowl of soggy Cheerios.

"Lawd Jesus is watching over your mama, Miss Annie, don't you worry."

"Honey, she'll be home in no time," Daddy said. "Try to eat your breakfast."

"Oh, Mr. Claiborne," Mae said, "when I saw that fire engine . . ."

"She inhaled a lot of smoke, Etha Mae, but there's no lung damage."

"Can we stay home from school?" Chris asked.

"I'm freezing," I said. "Can we close the windows now?"

"Lawd have mercy."

"It stinks in here!" Chris yelped.

"Son, let's go speak to the firemen."

———•———

I had an appointment with Dr. Verner that afternoon, but Daddy wanted me to cancel it. I had no intention of canceling. "I'll ride the bus."

"I'm going back to see your mother. I can take you on the way."

Mother was in an oxygen tent and only Daddy could visit at that point. In the car I turned on him when he commented on the weather. "Maybe it'll rain, Daddy. Maybe the sun won't ever shine again. Maybe a hurricane will blow down Atlanta! What are you going to do?"

"Moses is coming today. He's going to paint the den."

"About Mother! What about Mother? Daddy, I want to go stay with Ben. I don't want to live with y'all anymore."

"Do you believe me now, Dr. Verner? My mother's dangerous."

"Is she all right?"

"No, she's not all right! She's gonna burn herself up, or kill me, or all of us. Can you talk to my father? He won't *do* anything."

"I have spoken with him."

"You have?"

"He says your mother refuses treatment."

"She's sick. She needs help! No one, no one seems to understand that."

"He may not be willing to commit her."

"What's 'commit'?"

"Force her to go for inpatient treatment. There are legal steps."

"She'll be dead before he does that. We'll all be dead."

"Have your father call me, Sarah."

CHAPTER 22

Dr. Verner insisted I go back to school to keep my mind off of what was going on. I dreaded it. I despised the place, and was so behind in my work I'd never catch up.

"Well, it's about time, Claiborne."

"Hey, Ann."

"Where the hell have you been?" She stuffed her gym bag in the locker and shoved the door shut with her hip.

"We had a house fire."

"Really?"

"Yeah, we had to move out for awhile. What's going on?"

"I broke up with Bobby."

"I meant at your house."

Oh, that. Ancient history."

"Your parents still blame me?"

She looked away. "Who knows? They haven't said and I haven't asked. How's David?"

"We broke up."

"How come?"

I shrugged. Why go into it if we weren't "allowed" to be friends anymore. "Gotta go," I said. "See ya later."

Dr. Verner performed miracles with my father. While Mother sat under the oxygen tent, probably ordering nurses around, Dr. Verner met with Daddy and the doctor who'd seen her at Breen. He said Mother might harm herself—on purpose the next time—though he couldn't be sure. Daddy took him seriously.

"Your father will move her to the psychiatric unit there at Grady as soon as she's released from adult medicine," Dr. Verner told me.

"He committed her?"

"He's taking the steps."

"You don't know my mother. She'll walk out. You'll see!"

"She won't be able to, Sarah."

"Catherine's furious," Daddy said. "She wouldn't speak to me today."

"Do we have to go visit?"

"Her doctor would like to talk with you."

"Me? They still think I'm the crazy one, huh?"

"Honey, he's getting family history. I've talked with him."

"What about Ben? Is he going to give history? How 'bout Annie and Chris?

"They're too young."

Dr. Overstreet was nice and treated me like a grownup. He wrote on a pad when I answered his questions, but I could tell he was listening.

"Sarah, this isn't a test, so don't worry about rights and wrongs. Think carefully before you answer though, all right?"

Some questions I had to take a few minutes on, like did I remember a time when my mother seemed really happy. "One time, maybe."

"When was that?"

"I was little. We were up in the mountains and a man took us out in a motorboat. She liked being out there cruising on the lake, I could tell."

"It was relaxing."

"Yeah, but I ruined it."

"How was that?"

"I was lying on the dock watching the fish and fell in. Daddy had to save me."

"Did your mother punish you?"

"No! She said I scared her to death and hugged me because I was alive."

He smiled. "So you didn't spoil the day after all."

We spent an hour together and he thanked me. Daddy was waiting for me, and this time when he suggested stopping for ice cream on the way home, I said yes.

"I like Dr. Overstreet. I think *he* can make Mother better."

"I like him too, Sally. I hope your mother will keep seeing him."

I drank the melted strawberry ice cream out of the last bit of cone. "And if she won't, you can make her."

"No, honey."

"You committed her. Dr. Verner said you did. She has to stay!"

"She can only stay at Grady for seven days while they assess her. Then I'm hoping she'll agree to go back to Breen, or at least see Dr. Overstreet in his office."

"Those doctors at Breen didn't help her one bit. I don't get this. I thought you committed her!"

We were sitting in the car behind Liggett's Drug Store, and a man walking by stared. "Sshh. I did, sweetie, but they won't let her stay at Grady for more than a week. I can't force her to go to a private hospital, and if I commit her she'll be sent to Central State Hospital."

"Where?"

He hung his head. "The asylum in Milledgeville."

"Milledgeville? I thought that was for poor people . . .and murderers!"

"It's the state psychiatric facility."

My father asked me to go with him to meet with Dr. Overstreet at the end of the week. At first I had to sit in the waiting room while they talked. Daddy came out looking sad. "Sarah, your mother wants to come home. We've got to make a decision."

"Now?"

"Come on in, honey."

I asked Dr. Overstreet what he thought would happen if my mother came home. He said she would be all right *if* she took the medicine he'd prescribed.

"But what if she won't? What if she beats me again?"

"Sarah, it would be best if your mother agreed to therapy. She could live at home, stay on medication, see me—or someone else—on an outpatient basis."

"What about Milledgeville?"

"I don't think your father wants that."

I glared at Daddy and he looked away.

"Could they help her there, Dr. Overstreet?"

"I don't believe she'd receive the treatment she needs."

"What does she need? What's wrong with her?"

"She needs long-term psychotherapy. Your mother's frightened. Her mother died of breast cancer. Did you know that?"

"No, sir."

"She's convinced her cancer will recur. She's depressed, and, of course, the drinking exacerbates the depression."

"But she's not sad. Doesn't depressed mean sad? She's angry!

She's always furious . . . about everything. Mostly me!"

"We've had very little time with her, but we know there were abuse issues. Mrs. Claiborne said her father drank heavily after her mother's death. She recounted a time when he nailed her in a bathroom as a punishment."

"Mother lies all the time."

"It's not likely she made up the story, Sarah; she seemed ashamed to talk about it."

"Honey, Dr. Overstreet says Milledgeville is overcrowded," Daddy said. "There aren't enough doctors."

I wanted to scream. "What if she kills herself in our house? Or starts another fire?"

"Do you want me to put her in Milledgeville, Sally?"

"Mr. Claiborne, I'm not sure Sarah should have to make that decision."

"If she comes home, I'm running away." I charged out, banging the door shut behind me. I paced up and down the hall. My heart thumped hard in my chest and I felt light-headed. Dr. Overstreet said Mother couldn't get better at the hospital in Milledgeville, but I didn't want her to come home until she was better. If she did, and if I ran away, I'd worry about Annie and Chris—and Daddy. He wanted me to decide what to do, but I couldn't figure this out.

My mind whirred and my hands were shaking. I had to get out; I couldn't breathe.

I ran down the steps, through the parking deck, and came out on Marietta Street. Cars were backed up and honking. I walked fast toward Five Points, then kept going. One block, then another, and another. Maybe if I kept going and going I'd fall off the edge of the earth. For sure, I wasn't going back to Grady Hospital.

As I passed the Citizens and Southern Bank I felt better. I was thinking more clearly and my heart had slowed down. I planned to just keep walking until I could figure something out. In Dr. Overstreet's office I'd suddenly remembered that old movie *The Snake Pit*. I had watched it with Ben when I was ten or eleven and he was babysitting with us. It was about a woman who got locked up in an insane asylum. Whenever she smarted off with one of the doctors or nurses they'd hook wires to her head and shock her, or put her in a straightjacket. But the worst part was when they threw her down in a cellar with the really insane people, people screaming and moaning and writhing.

I shouldn't have watched that movie. I had nightmares about it for a week. Fortunately, Chris and Annie were asleep when we watched it.

My legs ached but I kept going. I'd walked all the way through the busy downtown area and was entering a shabby-looking neighborhood; I passed bars and warehouses and homeless men drinking from brown bags on the sidewalk. I just headed toward the sun, but it was disappearing fast. I wanted some water. I wanted to sit down. When I stood on a corner to rest, a man in a truck scared me. He was stopped at the red light. He stuck his tongue out at me and wriggled it in a disgusting way. "Need a ride, baby?" he asked, then spit tobacco juice at my feet.

I gritted my teeth and crossed the street in front of him. There was a run-down convenience store about a block down. I hurried in and ducked behind a shelf full of canned goods. A black man with watery eyes walked down the aisle and asked if he could help me. "No, thanks," I said. "Sorry. I don't see what I want." I practically ran out the door. The beat-up truck was nowhere in sight.

It was almost dark when I saw the Atlanta Water Works up ahead. Surely I could go in their office and use the restroom, get some water. But the gates were locked and there were only a few cars in the parking lot. I looked out at the huge reservoir, at all that water I couldn't get to. I plopped down right there on a grassy area by the main gate and cried.

Apparently, I fell asleep sitting there with my back against the chain link fence. The next thing I knew, I was looking up at the face of a man about my father's age. He was wearing a safari hat. "Are you lost, miss?"

"Uh, I guess so."

"Where you headed?"

I didn't answer.

"Do you want to call someone? I was just leaving, but I can take you in to use the phone."

"Take me in?"

"Sorry, miss. I'm D. J. Timmons; I work here at the waterworks."

He pointed at a plastic badge on his pocket. His face was kind. I didn't figure he was going to hurt me.

"If it's not too much trouble," I mumbled.

"Not a bit. We'll go right here to the maintenance office."

Daddy arrived in less than an hour, his shirt all wrinkled like he'd slept in it. He looked exhausted, but he hugged me. Mr. Timmons had stayed with me, made some business calls while I pretended to thumb through a magazine about golf. Daddy walked me out to the car, then went back to the office. I hoped he wasn't telling the man what was going on.

When he got in the car, he turned to me. "I know you're upset,

Sally, but you shouldn't have run out like that."

I hung my head. "I know, Daddy, but . . ." I started crying.

"I didn't call the police. I called them the last time you disappeared; I couldn't call them again."

He didn't sound angry. His voice was flat.

He pulled out and I assumed we were going home, but he got off the expressway at North Avenue and drove to the Varsity. "You haven't eaten all day."

I sniffed. "I can't eat."

"I'll get you a plain hotdog and chocolate milk. You'll feel better, honey."

He was right. My headache and nausea let up as I got the hotdog down. I was glad the Varsity served people out in their cars. With my red, puffy eyes I didn't want to run into someone I knew.

"I'm bringing your mother home tomorrow."

"Daddy, I—"

"Let me finish. I know what you're going to say." He looked out the window. When he turned back to me he took off his glasses and rubbed his eyes. I don't think I'd ever noticed my father's eyes before that night. And I'd known him all my life! Maybe it was because he wore glasses. Anyway, under the bright fluorescent lights outside, I could see that his eyes were a clear blue. True blue, you'd call them.

"Sally, I know you want me to commit your mother."

"No I don't!" He looked puzzled. "I don't want you to put her in the loony bin. Dr. Overstreet said it wouldn't help. Listen, I've got an idea. We'll move back to our old house, and—"

"Sarah."

"I can go back to North Atlanta where all my friends are."

"Your mother's coming home, and you and I are going to keep seeing Dr. Verner. We're going to work this out."

"Okay."

"I should never have asked you to make a decision like this. Now, I've made up my mind."

For some reason I didn't argue or whine or threaten. Somewhere along my long trek across downtown Atlanta and out Howell Mill, I gave up. I realized I could never "fix" my mother. And I couldn't live with Ben in his naked apartment with no TV, no comfortable chairs, me riding the bus named Desire back and forth to some ramshackle school. In a way, the fact that my father had finally made a decision was a relief.

After sleeping soundly all night—no nightmares, no dreams at all—I woke up feeling normal, maybe for the first time since Ben left. I hugged Daddy good morning in the kitchen.

I said I was going with him to get Mother. Etha Mae was bubbling over about "Miz Claiborne comin' home." She said her prayers had finally been answered. She thought Mother had been in the hospital all that time for smoke inhalation.

I rode up to the seventh floor on the elevator while Daddy searched for a parking spot. Mother was sitting in a chair in her robe; she looked surprised to see me but grinned.

"We were just talking about you! Sarah, this is Sue." She pointed at the nurse sitting in a straight-back chair beside her. "She's a reader!"

The woman smiled and started to speak to me, but Mother went on.

"Sue loves literature like we do. Look, she brought me these delightful short stories. How could I have missed Eudora Welty? Now, have your father go to the library and bring me everything she's written."

"But we're taking you home today, Mother."

Her eyebrows shot up. I guess no one told her she *had* to leave the hospital that day, or that Daddy had been thinking of sending her to Milledgeville. A wave of pity for her rolled over me.

"Oh! Well, of course," she mumbled. "What was I thinking?"

"Your mother told me all about your drawings," the nurse said. "She said you're real good. She said you're going to major in art in college."

I glanced at Mother; she looked dazed.

"Uh . . . probably," I said. "I'm not sure."

"I ought to buy a picture from you. When you get famous, it'll be worth a lot of money!"

Before I could speak, Mother popped back into the here and now. "You've been so wonderful to me, Sue. I'm certain Sarah would do something for you. What do you like? Landscapes? Seascapes? Don't you think we can come up with something, Sarah?"

"Um . . . sure, I'm sure we can. Oh, uh, Daddy's parking the car. He'll be up in a minute. I'll run get you a nice, cold Coke."

Walking down that long gray hall, I thought of my mother sitting back there in her pink silk nightgown and matching robe. And in that moment I knew in my bones that Daddy had made the right decision. Catherine Claiborne would never have survived in Milledgeville with all the wild-eyed, drooling crazies like the ones in *The Snake Pit*. Never, ever again would I push my father to commit her. That place wouldn't cure her; it would kill her.

*A*fter the fire and Mother's hospital stint, my father stopped taking so many business trips. Mother cold-shouldered him for weeks, but eventually seemed pleased to have him around. I can't say everything was Georgia-peachy at Westchester Circle, but some of Mother's venom had dried up. We got rattlesnake looks only now and then. Maybe knowing he had locked her up once and could do it again put the fear of Daddy in her.

Chris and Annie and I went back to public schools. I wanted to move back to our old neighborhood, but we didn't have to. Mother got special permission for us to attend schools outside our district. I imagine people at the school board still twitter about the day "that Claiborne woman" laid siege to their offices.

Laurie Riley and I picked up where we'd left off and stayed best friends until we went away to different colleges. She wore Roy's senior ring with a glob of wax to make it fit. I wore Alan Ray's St. Christopher medal, despite Mother's wisecracks about Catholics. Big Vick's brother Alan and I were inseparable, and David Blume hated it. But what could he do? He wasn't allowed to date Gentiles and I wouldn't convert to Judaism.

Mother cut back on her drinking, but refused to go for counseling or to take medication. She continued to "embroider the truth" (Dr. Verner's words). Not one soul in Atlanta knew she'd spent time in the psych ward at Grady; she told Amelia Martin she'd been touring Bellingrath Gardens in Mobile, Alabama. I heard her on the phone describing the vibrant hibiscus and various subtropical flowers. Soon other members of Dogwood Garden Club were calling to hear about her trip firsthand.

Dr. Verner said people everywhere lie, not just in the South, and always for the same reason—to be loved. I don't see how my mother telling people I made the honor roll when I didn't, or that Chris was his team's captain when he wasn't, would make people love her, but maybe she *believed* it would.

The main thing Dr. Verner advised was to humor Mother; she said it was necessary if I planned to live in the same house with her until I graduated. I did fairly well at it, although screaming matches still ensued and doors slammed; even Annie jumped in on occasion to demand a later curfew or to stick up for friends Mother blackballed. But the battlefield was often deserted and Mother got so bored she dusted off her Remington. During my senior year, she even wrote some feature stories for a neighborhood weekly.

Ben ended his standoff and flew to Atlanta for my graduation. Obviously, he needed support because he brought his girlfriend. Mother predicted she'd be a "trashy beatnik" he picked up in the French Quarter, but off the plane stepped pretty—and polite— Deborah Farwell. Needless to say, Mother clicked into high hostess gear and gushed over her day and night. It was hard on Deborah, but worked in my favor. As she toured Deborah around Atlanta, I had some time alone with my brother.

I told Ben what Gram had said about why our aunts and uncles ignore us, but he didn't buy it. "That's *her* theory," he said. "I think they're just busy. And, you know, they don't have a lot in common with Mother and Dad, really."

The hard part for me was talking about the choking and the beating and the fire, not to mention how I ran away—twice! "I kinda felt like I was going as crazy as she was," I told him.

He didn't say a word as I rattled on, one horror story after the other, but I could tell he was really hearing me. Not like in New Orleans when I tried to get through to him.

I never brought up the incident with Russell at his apartment. He'd mentioned earlier that Russell had moved to France and planned to stay; he was out of the picture. Besides, I was over it. I never thought about it anymore.

We took a little break and Ben made us ham sandwiches to eat out on the patio. He told me about courses he was taking at the University of New Orleans, and how he'd met Deborah. We chatted about light stuff for a while, but finally got to the topic of that long ago Christmas, the night Mother delivered her deadly lie. "I think she got drunk 'cause she was furious you were dropping out of Vandy," I said. "What would her friends say?"

"She was insisting I move home and go to Tech. There was no way. I couldn't go back to her ruling my life."

"Oh, I understand, Ben. I understand now." But I confessed that I had been furious with him for not coming home. "Didn't you believe me when I wrote about the hell we were going through here?"

"I knew what was going on. Dad called me almost every week, trying to convince me to come back."

"He did? He was talking to you all that time?"

"Yeah. He helped me with money a few times too. I knew things were bad, but what could I do?"

The talk was better than any we'd had before. He didn't act like I was a little kid anymore; in fact, he confided in me how hard Mother's lie had hit him, how depressed he'd been after the initial shock of it. "I looked in the mirror one night, about a week after I got to New Orleans. I looked in the mirror and there was nothing there."

"Oh, come on."

"I'm serious," he said. "I had no face."

"How about now? What do you see in the mirror now? Are you back?"

"Oh, yeah."

At one point during the weekend, Mother did lay out a land mine for Ben. Someone said something about crying at ceremonies like graduation; Mother said Ben wouldn't shed a tear. "He won't cry at my funeral either; I know that beyond a shadow of a doubt. That's why he adores that Camus book, *The Stranger*. Isn't that right, Ben? You identify with that man who didn't cry at his mother's funeral."

I could see a thick blue vein swelling in his neck. "Mother, Ben hated *The Stranger*," I said. "I'm the one who asked for it for Christmas. I loved those mask-like faces on the cover."

Deborah caught on and swept in to help. "We looked all over the Quarter for that edition, didn't we, Ben?"

Our diversionary tactic worked and Mother launched into a discussion of where to go for dinner after my graduation. Ben smiled and kicked me under the dinner table like in the old days.

The graduation ceremony itself was surreal. As I walked away from the stage with my diploma, I spotted my family. With Chris standing up in his seat, I couldn't miss them. Strung out across a row near the front were Ben and Deborah, Daddy, Mother, Annie, Etha Mae, and Chris. They were all smiling and clapping except Etha Mae, who was, of course, weeping and dabbing her nose with a big white handkerchief. Mother wasn't scowling at Ben or cutting her eyes at him. This was a new picture, one I planned to keep stored in my head.

Afterward, Alan and I and Laurie and Roy went to a class party at the downtown Holiday Inn. I was able to stay out late because I was spending the night at Laurie's. Mother, of course, had protested, said I should "be with family," but I won that battle. I guess she was scared to act too crazy in front of Deborah.

Laurie drove me home on Sunday at noon. Mother had fixed a huge brunch: cheese grits, scrambled eggs, bacon, fresh fruit cup, and homemade coffee cake. I was flabbergasted; she must have gotten up at dawn.

Chris took off on his bike when we'd finished, and Mother begged me to bring out my sketchbook to show Deborah and Ben what I'd been working on all year. "Let's relocate to the living room," she chirped as Daddy and Annie began clearing the table.

"Please let me help," Deborah said. It wasn't a fake gesture; she was already picking up dishes.

"Absolutely not, dear. But thank you."

The phone rang and Daddy came out of the kitchen.

"Catherine, it's Amelia. Should I take a message?"

"No, no, I'll take it in the den."

I didn't want to bore Ben and Deborah with my artwork, but I went to my room to get my portfolio—to avoid an argument, to humor Mother as Dr. Verner had instructed. Heading back to the living room, I passed the den, then stopped for a minute to eavesdrop.

Yes, Amelia. Oh, the ceremony was lovely. But I wish they'd held it somewhere else; that old municipal auditorium is horribly run down.

He certainly did! And he brought his beautiful bride-to-be. We were thrilled; we'd heard so much about her.

Oh, I can't think about a rehearsal dinner now! I'm trying to get Sarah ready for college. She needs a totally different wardrobe for Florida.

Yes, Sarasota. Honestly, she wanted to stay here, but I said, "Sarah, Ringling is such a fine school. You ought to feel privileged to be going there."

Well, of course I'll miss her, but she'll be home for Thanksgiving. We'll all be here together!

The End

ACKNOWLEDGMENTS

Special thanks . . .

To the team at Archer Hill Publishing for their enthusiasm and expertise.

To my writers' group colleagues for their helpful critique, especially Lana Hendershott and Elizabeth Watson, who read the "almost final" draft and provided valuable feedback.

To Gelia Dolcimascolo, Atlanta poet, author, and writing instructor extraordinaire, for daring me to write my first short story almost two decades ago.

To the many writers' organizations in North Carolina that make this state an oasis for authors and poets, among them the NC Arts Council, the NC Writers' Network, and the Writers' Workshop of Asheville. Through their grants, contests and awards, workshops and conferences, these groups are vital to the writing community.

To my librarian sister, Nancy Snowden, who has generously shared tips on researching and fact-checking with me over the years.

To my brother and sister-in-law, Fraser and Dian Snowden, and my "soul brothers" Randy Shepherd and Tom Jones, who have encouraged me and applauded my successes along the way.

And, finally, to Colin, Lynnae, and Aedan Palmer—my son, daughter-in-law, and grandson—for their joie de vivre and creativity. They inspire me.

This project was supported by
a Regional Artist Project Grant from the Asheville Area Arts Council
and the North Carolina Arts Council, a state agency.